SOMEONE TO CALL BAE 2

SIREN

Cole Hart
SIGNATURE NOVELS

Someone To Call Bae 2

Copyright © 2021 by Siren

All rights reserved.

Published in the United States of America.

Mailing List

PREVIOUSLY...
JAYA

It was almost dusk, the sun was starting to wane, and that was the only reason I was outside in this Miami weather. The one thing I loved about the townhome that Ice and I shared was that it had a covered pool out back.

Ice was barbecuing all my favorite foods and my fat ass couldn't wait to smash. Somehow our dinner for two turned into party when Shawnie and Dejah came through. I was so happy that two of the most important men in my life were getting along, because I still wasn't fucking with my daddy. He didn't want me with Isaiah but couldn't give me a reason why. I was over it. If he didn't want to be happy for me, then fuck him. The one person that should be mad is Shawnie and if he could accept my relationship with Ice than I didn't see why my dad couldn't.

So, if Shawnie could be supportive of my relationship, then I could do the same for my cousin. If Shawnie wanted to be with Dejah I was going to be happy for him. Dejah seemed cool and I was willing to be cordial for Shawnie's sake.

"I love the ring." I commented on Dejah's beautiful engagement ring.

"Thank you!" Dejah gushed as she held up her ring for me and Ice to see.

"Nothing but the best for my bay bae!" Shawnie kissed Dejah.

All my life I had never seen Shawnie affectionate. He cared but he wasn't about to hug and kiss. He could barely say I love you. I didn't know who this man was that stood in front of me, but I loved to see Shawnie happy. He deserved it because I've seen my big cousin go through hell. Prison, going through it with Keisha, his dad dying in a bad car accident and having to watch over my wild ass. Dejah was really good for him, and I was here for it.

"Aww shit bro. That's real nice." Ice smiled as he looked at Dejah's ring.

"Dejah, who did your braids?" I admired Dejah's hair.

"My homegirl, Shanice."

"You think she can do some Coi Leray knotless goddess braids?" I wondered. I wanted something cute and different for my gender reveal coming up.

"Yes. She is the truth. She is off on Tuesdays and Fridays, so hit her up."

"Yes, give me her number. Give me yours too. I'ma send you an invite to the gender reveal." I smiled.

"Okay." Dejah smiled.

Two Weeks Later

"When you said the girl could do hair, you didn't say the shit was going to be ghetto." I texted Dejah.

"She a little hood. What happened? LOL"

"Two words. Weed man. I'll call you when I get done."

In the last two weeks me and Dejah been kicking it tough. I'm going to always love Keisha, but Dejah was cool as fuck. If I wasn't with her, I was with Ice or at the food truck. Plus, seeing my cousin so happy was the best feeling. I had found love and so had Shawnie.

But Dejah's friend was a different story. I was hood but this bitch was straight ghetto. I understood life happened. But I had been here for over two hours. So far Shanice had fried up some chicken for me, her, and her fourth baby daddy. I mean the chicken was fire and my fat ass loved to eat. But I was here to get my hair braided. We drove to the weed man's house so that she could get her baby daddy, Kevin, some gas. The actual time she did my hair, her baby was hollering and I ended up having to hold him.

"You want me to curl the ends at the bottom?" Shanice asked as she looked at her progress of the three braids in my head.

"Yes-

"Hold on. Ahjalik! Laniya! You see me sitting here. Get in the car!" Shanice yelled as she honked her horn.

I didn't feel comfortable sitting in another woman's man's face. So, when it was time for Shanice to get her two oldest kids from school I hopped in the car. At this point I was invested. In the hours I'd been at Shanice's house I met her mama, two of her siblings, the fourth baby daddy, and her weed man. Shit my ass was practically family the way she included me into everything. Reid Elementary was swarming with kids for the after school let out. Two cute little girls came running to the car and I was hoping if I had a daughter that she was just as pretty as Shanice's daughters. As ghetto as Shanice was her daughters were dressed cute and their hair was elaborately braided.

"Hi mama! Who is she?" One of the girls spoke as she got to the car.

"My client. Laniya don't be rude. Say hi."

"Hi."

"Hi." Ahjalik spoke too as they both got in the car.

"Hi." I responded as Shanice took off back to her house.

These Coil Leray braids should not have taken this long considering that it was no more than twelve braids. And after three hours I still only had three braids in my head. At this point I just wanted to get it done. Once Shanice finally got done with my head, I was in love with my hair and she only charged me

$60. As much time as it took, I was still going to continue to fuck with Shanice for my hair.

"What do you think of my hair?" I asked Ice when he came to pick me up from Shanice's house.

"I love it." Ice spoke as he stared at my head.

"You figure out what you going to wear for tomorrow?" I asked.

"I got this blue Stefano Ricci shirt and some white jeans."

"Blue?" I rolled my eyes. "You want a boy. I thought we were team girl."

"Hell naw! You see how bad my little sisters are. Grown ass men trying to get with my baby. Hell no. Could you imagine if she was pretty like you? Man, I'm killing every nigga. I don't need that stress."

I couldn't contain my laughter because if it wasn't for Shawnie I would have been on my hot girl summer shit every day when I was younger. "She isn't going to be that bad." I tried to reassure Ice.

"I know she's not. Because she is a he."

"Whatever. Either way I'm naming the baby Israel Isaiah Green if it's a boy. Israel I'Liana Green if it's a girl." I grinned at Ice.

"That's a lot of I's. I thought you was going at least give the baby, Trap Star's last name." Ice glanced over at me.

"Why? He ain't the father." I did my part in telling Trap Star that I was pregnant. He said he was going to come down to Miami and never showed up. Maybe he was scared of Shawnie. But he wasn't scared of Shawnie when he was texting me for us to meet up for some pussy. I had to block his ass. He wasn't worried about the baby, so there was no reason for me to continue to communicate with him.

"I told him. He doesn't give a fuck. We're moving on." I dared not tell Ice that Trap Star was trying to fuck.

"So, Israel for both a girl and boy?"

"Yup." I rubbed on my stomach. I wanted a "I" name for my

first love to match my forever love. "Where we going?" I noticed that Ice missed our exit on the highway.

"You will see."

The next thing I knew we was in South Beach at the Miami Edition Hotel. The shit was nice. I needed this mini baecation and spending some time from home even if it was only for one night.

I was already feeling insecure since I was gaining weight and I was starting to waddle a little bit. I was all stomach and this was one big ass baby.

"Damn you waddle so sexy." Ice commented as I came out the bathroom.

"Nigga, bye." I rolled my eyes.

"I'm so serious. Bring yo sexy fat ass here."

"So, you sayin' that I belong on 600 pound life?" I caught a fake attitude.

"No." Ice snatched me into his space since he was sitting down. I didn't move as Ice rubbed on my stomach. All I was wearing was a bra and Ice laid me on my side on the bed.

Ice brought out some massage oil and began to rub my body down. Low key this shit was better than sex. I didn't even realize my back hurt until Ice rubbed his strong hands across it.

"Isaiah?" I called out as I closed my eyes.

"Hmm?"

"I'm about to be knocked out. So, if you were trying to smash, you're going to have to catch me in the a.m." I yawned.

"You sound like a whole nigga."

I know I did. Because that's what I was raised around. I low key had to remind myself that I was a female. "I'm working on it." I commented before falling asleep.

❂❀❂

I was so excited to find out the gender of my baby today. I had no complaints about life right about now and to be honest, I was just happy to be having a healthy baby. I was making decent money at the food truck, I had Shawnie, I had my auntie, I had Dejah, and more importantly I had Ice.

Who would have thought that after all these years apart, that I would fall in love with Ice? That my high school crush would one day become the man of my dreams.

"You like?" I came out the bathroom to model my flowy tropical dress in soft pinks and grays.

Ice smiled as he took in my maternal glow. "You look good babe." Ice's hand went straight to my ass.

"I'm not changing again, Isaiah." I stepped back. I'd been up since six this morning fucking and sucking. As soon as I have this baby, I was getting on birth control. Ice wasn't about to have me pregnant every nine months. I wanted to give him a baby, but I wanted my body to heal first.

It was only 11:30 in the morning and I had finally got Ice to leave me alone and get dressed.

"I'ma leave you alone...for now." Ice kissed me before grabbing his shirt off the bed.

"I'm hungry." I complained as my baby kicked me to let me know they were hungry too. "What time is check out?"

"In thirty minutes. You can't wait to we get to my mom's? The party starts at 1pm."

I looked at Ice like he lost his mind.

"Alright, but just the drive thru. We don't have time for no sit down and eat shit."

"Ok I want some Zaxby's."

"That's an hour drive. No! You want Checkers' or some McDonald's?"

"I want Zaxby's though." I pouted.

"McDonald's or Checkers?" Ice replied not giving a fuck I was on the verge of crying.

"McDonald's." I responded as few tears slipped from my eyes. This baby had me crying about the most stupid ass shit. I was thug and here I was crying about some damn fast food. One day didn't go by without me crying. I became a punk ass cry baby. I hated that shit.

Unlike Shawnie, Ice was sensitive to my tears. "If you still want Zaxby's, I will take you after the gender reveal. Alright?" Ice gently wiped my tears from my eyes.

"Okay." I tried to smile but Ice being nice made me want to cry more.

Bitch, get it together.

I smashed my Big Mac in the car before Ice and I pulled up to Miss Tia's house. When your baby's adoptive grandma is the plug, they go all the way out. There was a huge sign in the yard that read, "Will it be a girl or a boy?" Then in the driveway there was an even bigger marquee sign that said, "Baby Green" with a macaron pink, pale blue, and metallic silver balloon garland. This was just the outside of the house; I could only imagine the inside and the back yard.

"Yo mama did her thing!" I got excited getting out the car.

"She really did." Ice grabbed my hand as we made our way into the house.

As soon as I got in the house, I saw my family, Ice's big ass family and Ice's friends. Even Dejah and Shanice came and I was happy to see them since they were slowly becoming my friends.

"Girl, hook me up with Lil' Way." Shanice spoke as soon as she got me and Dejah alone.

"What happened to Kevin?" Dejah questioned.

That was what I was thinking.

"Fuck him! He violated his parole. His stupid ass went to go see his parole officer with his gun on him." Shanice rolled her eyes. "He on his way back to prison. Is Lil' Way single?"

"I think. But he a hoe."

"What did Kevin Gates say? Me too!"

"Bye!" Dejah looped her arm into mine and steered me away from Shanice.

"Fuck y'all!" Shanice called behind us.

"I'm ready to see what this baby is going to be." My Aunt

Keyonna said as Shanice, Dejah and me walked into the back yard.

"Me too!" Ice grabbed my hand. "Come on baby."

Ice led me to a huge black box in the middle of the yard as everyone began to gather around us. I was so nervous. Shawnie, Ice, Miss Tia, Lil' Way, and Isis was team boy. While me, Indica, Dejah, Auntie Keyonna, and Shanice was team girl. I couldn't wait to find out my baby's sex.

"1...2..."

"Isaiah Green you are the father!"

Everyone turned to see Trinity standing there in the crowd. I was ready to pop off on Ice's ex-girlfriend for crashing my gender reveal. But my eyes fell to the tummy that was bigger than mine.

Everybody stood frozen as Trinity kept talking. "I don't know why y'all so happy for Jaya. That's not Isaiah's baby. But this one is." Trinity rubbed her stomach.

"Isaiah what the fuck is going on?" Miss Tia questioned. "Is that your baby?"

So, it was true. My dad was right. I was the side bitch. I believed Ice when he said that he wasn't cheating. But the nigga had a whole baby on the way. We playin' house and he already got a family. I wanted to swing on both Trinity and Ice. But what was the point? He was her man first.

I didn't speak as I tried to leave. "Jaya!" Ice tried to grab me.

"You stayed in my face, saying you wasn't cheating." I cried, my tears blurring my vision.

"I'm not. Baby hear me out..."

"There's nothing to say!"

"Jay"... Ice couldn't finish his statement as Shawnie came out of nowhere punching Ice in the face. I didn't even want to stick around as everybody tried to break up the fight. I was back where I started...A cheating ass nigga.

The words were on repeat in my head. The same way you got him is the same way you going to lose him.

But I didn't know that the shit was going hurt this much.

ICE

NOW THAT WE ARE ALL CAUGHT UP....

"Can I talk to you?" Trinity asked as I tried to call Jaya for the umpteenth time.

"There ain't shit to talk about." I dismissed Trinity.

"You have reached, 7..8..6" Jaya's voicemail spoke as I hung up.

"I'm having your baby Isaiah."

"Bitch you lying. I ain't smashed for a minute." I tried to ignore Trinity.

"No Jaya's baby ain't yours. But I'm carrying your son." Trinity got snappy.

I didn't have time for this bullshit. I wasn't fucking Trinity and I ain't been fucking Trinity since right before the food truck opened. She could miss me with that shit. I needed to find my keys so I could go find my bitch.

"Don't think I won't tell my dad how you been acting!" Trinity yelled from behind me as I walked back towards the house.

"Bitch, fuck you and yo daddy." I remembered that my keys was sitting on the island in my mother's kitchen.

"Jayson Mitchell is my dad."

A nigga was already light skinned and the little bit of color I had, had drained from my face. "What the fuck did you say?"

"You been fucking my sister, Isaiah. You should really watch who you deal with. You thought my dad was really tripping about you fucking Jaya. No, he was pissed that you was fucking both of his daughters."

A nigga didn't even know how to respond to that. Trinity and Jaya didn't even look alike. I had not an inkling that I had smashed sisters. I was only with Trinity for a month, fucked the bitch only three times. I didn't know who her family was. And I for sure wasn't trying to be a family with her.

I was really feeling like both her and her bitch ass daddy had set me up. Because who the fuck waits months to say they pregnant? Hearing Trinity's voice, she was the bitch that was playing on my phone. She knew about Jaya's baby not being biologically mine because Jayson told her. Jaya only had Shawnie, Keyonna, and her dad. And the only person that knew Trinity was Jayson.

I knew Jayson was foul but I didn't know he was moving like that. He had a whole other daughter, and nobody knew about that shit. I was starting to wonder if he told Trinity to get at me to keep ties on me. But the pussy was trash, so she wasn't ever going to be the one. I wasn't claiming no baby without no DNA and my only concern was getting my bitch back.

"You ain't got nothing to say?" Trinity rubbed on her stomach. "You going to be here for me and our baby?"

"I ain't claiming shit until I get a DNA test. Ain't shit changed between me and you. I don't fuck with you, Trinity, and if you thought trapping me with a baby was going make me be with you, you only played yourself." I walked back into my mother's house, leaving Trinity looking stupid in the front yard.

I already knew that when I went back into the house, me and Shawnie was going to go toe to toe. But I needed to find my girl. Shawnie was like my brother, and I hated that it had to come to this. I wasn't no scary nigga and Shawnie had hands. But I did too. However, when came to Jaya, I would go to war with her whole family. That was my bitch, and I wasn't letting no one come between us, including my possible baby mama aka Jaya's sister.

This shit was too ghetto.

2

SHAWNIE

"**W**here you at?" I questioned as Jaya finally picked up the phone.

"I'm in the Uber...

"Change the route to my house. I'm about to come get you."

"I don't want to have to come back to your house." Jaya sobbed. "I keep fucking up and you got to keep saving me."

Usually I was an asshole, but my cousin was hurting so I was hurting. "Fuck all that! I got you no matter what. You hear me?"

"Why would Ice do me like this?" Jaya cried.

"Because he a bitch. Every time I see the nigga it's going to be a problem." And I meant that shit.

The few blows that Ice and I got in had cause some damage. My lip was busted, and Ice's eye was black. I was trying to knock that nigga out. But everyone was trying to break up the fight hollering, we best friends. On my mama, fuck that nigga. If you were going to be knocking down all these bitches, he should've left Jaya out of it.

I was still at Ice's mama's house. But I was ready to bounce now that I knew of my cousin's whereabouts.

"Is she alright?" Ma Dukes asked.

"Where she at?" Ice had the nerve to ask.

"Bitch, worry about your shone! My cousin is good." I got angry all over again.

"Fuck that bitch. I'm only worried about Jaya." Ice dismissed me.

"Y'all been best friends since y'all was fifteen." Mama T tried to interject. Ice's mom ain't never been soft but I could tell that she was bothered by me and Ice's falling out.

I didn't want to be involve with this shit and one of the reasons I didn't want Jaya fucking with none of my boys. Because if shit went left, I would have to choose a side. I'm going to always side with my cousin, right, wrong, or indifferent. But Ice was dead wrong for this shit. I was a nigga and before shit got serious with me and Dejah, I was knocking down every bitch that came my way. But I had them hoes in line. Plus, Ice made a commitment to Jaya and he fuckin' on some thirsty bitch. I don't even look at my cousin on no incest shit, but this Trinity bitch had nothing on Jaya. He had definitely downgraded.

As much as I wanted to put hands on Ice, I didn't want to continue to disrespect Mama T or my mama. "She's fine. She said she going to get a room for a few days." I lied. "Baby you ready?" I asked Dejah.

"You go handle what you need to handle. I'm going to just go home." Dejah gave me my space.

I appreciated it, but I wanted to be around my girl. "No, come with me. I need you." I smiled but my grin was drenched in lust.

Dejah knew what it was. "Okay."

"Shawnie I need to holler at you." Ice tried to get my attention.

"I'm good, Zo. You got you a baby on the way. Broke Jaya's heart and shit. There ain't shit you got to say to...

"Trinity is Jayson's daughter." Ice blurted out.

There was a gasp that spread across everybody that stood in the kitchen. At this point I wasn't shocked of nothing Uncle Jayson was doing. My Uncle was doing the most. And while I didn't publicly talk about his actions, I knew his ass was in the wrong. If he was willing to lie to my face and say that Jaya and Ice was siblings, he was bound to say anything and do anything. I wouldn't be surprised if he told me that bullshit ass lie to make sure that I stayed on Jaya's hat about fucking with Ice. My uncle was wrong for keeping he had another daughter from us, but Ice should not have been fucking on both of them.

"Damn. That's fucked up." I hid my emotions. I was going to holler at my uncle ASAP. I just wasn't into bringing family business to everybody. Whatever was going on I needed to holla at him in private. "Dejah, you ready...

"JaShawn did you know about this?" My mom questioned.

"No. Uncle Jayson been moving different and now I'm wondering what the fuck is really going on."

"Bro I ain't do Jaya dirty. I ain't trying to point fingers but your uncle is the reason why shit is fucked up. I smashed Trinity before I got with Jaya. I been cut her off. I don't know what is going on with Trinity and Jayson but I been nothing but real."

"My bad." I hugged it out with my bro. I was looking at Ice as a grimy ass nigga and the whole time he wasn't doing shit. My mother's brother wasn't tripping with me per se, but he was bringing distress to by baby cousin. Jaya may have been my cousin but we were raised as siblings and I played no games about her. This nigga sat behind a jail cell while I was protecting his daughter. If anything, I was the damn daddy. My mom did her best for both of us, but it was my ass buying $100 Jordans and making sure her ass stayed on the right track.

"I get it." Ice replied. If muthafuckas thought we was going to be having some Lifetime movie moment, they were mistaken. "Do you know where Jaya's at?"

"Call her." It was up to Jaya if she wanted to see him. "I'ma take Dejah home."

"Get at me later bro."

And just like that, Ice and I's beef was squashed.

"It's a girl." I relayed to Ice.

"Fuck." Ice rubbed his hands down his face, but I saw a smile creep on his face.

"Her ass ain't going to be able to do shit though. We going to be on her ass. Congrats bro on the baby girl." Ice had my approval to be my niece's dad.

"Thanks. Real shit. Let me go find Jaya. I'm get at you. "

"Bet."

"Shawnie...you're so nasty." Dejah cooed as I walked behind her as I slipped my hand in her shorts.

"But you like it." I commented as we walked up the stairs of my apartment. "What the fuck?" My eyes fell on Keisha as she stood in front of my door.

Ever since she called me and told me that Tommy had set us up. I haven't talked to her. I'm not going to front; I was avoiding her. I was torn between who I was going to choose. But I was leaning towards Dejah because she had never turned her back on me. As much as I loved Keisha, I wasn't about to break Dejah's heart. I loved her too.

"You been ignoring my calls, Shawnie?" Keisha questioned.

"Baby, go in the house... I turned to Dejah because I didn't want any drama.

"The only thing she needs to do is leave." Keisha stepped forward as I seen her hands ball up in a fist. "You were my man first."

I wasn't about to let Keisha put her hands on Dejah. Dejah was a good girl and Keisha was like me, she loved to fight.

"Keisha just leave Zo...

"Nope. I been through too much shit with your ass. I'm not about to let this basic bitch get what belongs to me."

Dejah started to laugh. "Girl, Shawnie ain't going nowhere." Dejah flashed her engagement ring. "You may have had the bond, but I got the ring. And it didn't take his whole life to figure that out."

"You just mad that he still got to think of my pussy just to nut."

"And yet he still proposed to me. Shawnie upgraded. Go back to your busted nigga, dusty bitch."

Keisha wasn't the arguing type and it surprised me that the bickering went this long. Before I could react, Keisha's fist was connecting with Dejah's face. I really wasn't inspecting Dejah to swing back. As mellow as Dejah is, she was able to hold her own. Keisha must have been surprised too because Keisha froze for half a second. Then her crazy ass started swinging like she was a nigga and I had to end this fight.

I snatched up Dejah and put her behind me. "Naw, Shawnie let her ass fight! Because I'm not going nowhere. This hoe is temporary and you know it!" Keisha yelled trying to get to Dejah, but I wasn't having it.

"Bitch ain't no one scared of you!" Dejah shouted but she wasn't about that life. If I would have let her keep going, Keisha was going to beat her ass.

"Chill, Dejah." I barked. I was trying save her ass and she was trying to have Keisha fuck her up. Dejah piped down as she took a few steps back.

"Shit ain't changed Kesh! You still were fucking the opps." Granted, Keisha left the state to save me. But what about when a nigga was sitting in a prison cell and her ass was laid up with Tommy. In this moment I had made my decision. I was staying with Dejah. She met me in prison and didn't once switch up on me. Tommy, that bitch ass nigga at her job, all tried to smash, and my bitch stayed loyal. So why the fuck would I give up on Dejah. When Keisha could be led off by a broke ass nigga.

"It's over, Zo. I appreciate you for looking out for me. But this shit wouldn't have gotten this bad if you weren't fucking with Tommy. Come on babe." I led Dejah to my front door.

Keisha stood there as the tears fell and I knew that both of us would never be the same.

"You got to think about Keisha, when you nut?"

I wiped my hands down face as I fell back onto the couch. When I was fucking all kinds of bitches, I didn't have to deal with this shit. And now a nigga trying to do right and be with one bitch and now it's a problem.

"Please don't start." I kept my eyes closed. "I find out my new cousin is pregnant by my cousin's man, my uncle is on some grimy shit and now this bullshit?"

"Do you have to think about your ex to fuck me?" Dejah stood over me, ignoring everything I just said.

"No!" I spoke truthfully.

"If there's nothing there, why she poppin' off like that. You still fucking her?"

"No."

"You still love her?"

"I'm not about to do this shit." I didn't want to lie to her, but at the same time I didn't want to hurt her feelings.

"Wow!" Dejah stepped back. "You do love her?"

"I wish I could turn off my feelings." I looked up at Dejah. "But she been in my life since I was eight years old. I'm twenty-five. So, the connection is there. But I love you..."

"So, you still want her?"

"Dejahnae, I want you. I choose you. Who did I give the ring to?"

"But who has your heart?" Dejah's eyes began to water.

My voice was stuck in my throat because as much I was for Dejah and as dirty Keisha did me, she still had my heart. And sadly, I don't think that as much of a good woman Dejah was, she wasn't going to able to change my feelings.

❧ 3 ❧

JAYA

I didn't know where Shawnie was, but as much as I appreciate him letting me stay at his house, that air mattress was not the business. I was going to get a hotel room for few days, because I needed to figure out what I was going to do. I told myself when I moved back to Miami that I was going to get a job and take care of myself.

But what do I do? Get involved with another cheating drug dealer, become dependent and when shit hit the fan, I'm the one that is looking stupid. I had to do better for me and my baby. As much as I loved Shawnie, he couldn't continue to take care of me or rescue me from when I fucked up. I had to realize that I attracted toxic niggas.

The short time I was with Ice I saved my money; I be damned if I walk away with nothing. I wasn't planning on leaving Ice today. So instead of going to the hotel, I was going to the house to get my car, and my belongings.

"Can we talk?" I heard Ice behind me as I packed up my shit.

I knew that if I turned around, I wouldn't have the nerve to leave. I hated that even though I was through with Ice, I was still in love with him. It wasn't the same when I broke up with

Trap Star. I accepted that our marriage was over, but this? I was going to be fucked up for a while.

I quickly wiped my tears from my eyes and spoke. "I wish you nothing but the best Isaiah, with your baby and your baby mama." I tried to keep my voice even, but it was cracking from the tears.

"Thank you." Ice wrapped his arms around me. "But you are more than my baby mama and my daughter...

"Trinity is having a girl?" I felt my heart breaking as I tried to break away from Ice's grip, but he held me tighter. Not only was Trinity having Ice's first child, but it was also the daughter that I wanted with him.

"No, we are." Ice turned me around to face him. "I'm not cheating baby. I love you, Jaya. But I got something to tell you."

This was it. Ice was realizing that I was more of burden. "You want to be with Trinity?" I searched Ice's eyes for clarity.

"Trinity is your sister."

I was so confused. "What you mean she is my sister?" I shouted.

"She's your dad's daughter. Remember when that chick called saying I was smashing?"

I remembered very well. I shook my head up and down.

"That was her. You know I ain't been no hater. But your dad has been behind that shit with Gio, telling Trinity that I wasn't the bio dad of Israel and shit, most of our problems. Your dad been throwing shade because he doesn't want to see us together. I don't know the whole story, but it has a lot to do with Trinity being your sister."

I was feeling like the ground was going to come from under me and I needed to sit down to process what Ice had just told me. I moved away from Ice and plopped down on the bed. I didn't see the resemblance between me and Trinity. But for my dad to keep this from me was a blow to the gut. But there were bigger matters that I needed to deal with. "Is Trinity carrying your baby?"

Ice let out a deep breath of frustration. "I don't know. But what I do know is that my love for you and our baby hasn't wavered."

"If this is your baby," I swallowed hard. Just thought of it made me sick. "Then what?"

"I'm take care of my son."

"My sister is giving you a boy?" I smirked sarcastically. Even though I wanted a daughter, Ice really wanted a boy. I wanted to be the one to give him that gift, but my sister had beat me to the punch. I really had a sister. Something I always wanted. But not in the capacity of her being my man's baby mama. Could shit get any more ghetto.

"I don't know. But if he's mine, I'ma raise him along with my daughter."

I stood corrected about it not getting any more ghetto. Ice was willing to raise both kids by two sisters.

"I can't do this Ice. I just can't." I stood up. "I love you. I do. But this is too much for me. If this is your baby, then he is both my nephew and my stepson. Regardless, whether you are the father or not, he is still my daughter's cousin." I was crying because I wanted to be with Ice, but I chose to sleep with another woman's man, and these were the consequences. Weird fucked up consequences but none the less the consequences.

"Jaya." Ice grabbed me by my hands. I ain't never seen this nigga cry. But the tears were welling up in his eyes. "I'm not trying to hurt you. But I can't do this without you. I'm sick without you. Shit, a nigga can't breathe without you. I fell in love the first time I seen you. Mean ass girl with the bright red hair." Ice reminiscence about the first time we met back when I was thirteen. "You said, nigga don't be banging on my door like that.' I was there to see Shawnie but after that I couldn't stop thinking about you..."

I remember exactly what Ice was referring to. He had come to my house looking for Shawnie and I was mad that he was knocking like he was the police. In less than two years Ice was giving me my first kiss and he was the first to ever rub his hand in between my legs. I wanted him to be my first, but I was so scared that Shawnie would fuck me up. From the time I was thirteen all the way up to seventeen Ice had been someone I cared about. I just knew it wasn't going to work because of Shawnie, so right before I met Trap Star I cut Ice off completely. I was in love with him, shit I still am, but back then I didn't want him having to lose his friendship with Shawnie because of me.

"I know. I never stopped thinking about you either." I truthfully spoke. Because even though I was married to Trap Star I still thought about Ice constantly.

"So baby, if this love story has been going on since I was fifteen and you was thirteen, why are we going to let anybody stop it? First you stop fucking with me because of Shawnie, then you married Trap Star. You didn't think that shit had me feeling some type of way? And now this shit. You are saying you can't do this. And I'm saying that I can't lose you again. I'm willing to go to war with your whole family behind you. I don't give a fuck about how Shawnie, your dad or Trinity feels. I love you Jaya." Ice's voice got loud.

"I don't know how I'm going to do all this." I cried. "I shouldn't have never fucked with another woman's man. I shouldn't have broken up with you because I was scared to disappoint my cousin."

"We can't change the past. But I can't live my future without you babe. You say you don't know how you're going to do this, and I don't know either. What I do know is we are going to do it together." Ice kissed my forehead as I closed my eyes letting the tears fall. "You my bae for life." Ice whispered in my ear before crashing his soft lips against mine.

"You my bae for life." I repeated the words.

"We had a stressful day and that shit ain't good for you or Israel. Let's put all the bullshit to the side and enjoy our weekend. You still want that Zabxy's?"

"No...yes." I rolled my eyes with a smile on my face.

"Mean ass. Come here." Ice brought me closer, slipping his hands in between my thighs. "You know daddy is hungry too."

"Nasty ass." I smiled. "I don't want to be stuck in the car for two hours. Let's just get food here."

"I got a better idea. Let's go down to the Keys." Ice wrapped his arms around me as his hands fell to my ass.

"Uh-huh." I was listening.

"With a hot tub, room service, turn off our phones and just enjoy the fact that we are having a beautiful daughter."

I was all smiles. "Yes, I love it."

❦ 4 ❦

TRINITY

I had been blowing up Isaiah's phone since Jaya's gender reveal party. First it was going to voicemail and now it was disconnected. I was hot. You would have thought that the news of me being pregnant with his first baby would have had him running to do right, but he was so worried about my bitch of a sister. What did this bitch have that I didn't?

Jaya was a hood bitch, recently divorced, pregnant, homeless, no college degree, and a hoe and yet Isaiah wanted her over me. The woman who had a degree in political science, never married, and I wasn't a hoe. If Isaiah would have let me, I could have him sitting with the mayor, the governor, and members of city council. Miami could have been his oyster. He didn't have to sell drugs anymore but rather be the Stedman to my Oprah.

I knew all my life that Jaya was my sister, I was eight years old when my dad went to prison. He was with my mother and out of nowhere some trifling bitch named Maya comes saying that she is having my father's child. The bitch even named her bastard daughter after my father. My mother was devasted. Maya was a home wrecker just like her slut of a daughter.

But despite Jayson being married to my mom, he kept it a secret from his family. But he had no problem prancing that little bitch around while my mother and I stayed in the shadows like some side bitches.

My father and mother's marriage was arranged by my grandfather. If my dad wanted to be the kingpin of the dope world, he had to do right by my mom when she got pregnant with me. I learned early that my parents' marriage was a marriage born out of duty rather than love. My mom Kimberly told me in a drunken state that Maya was my father's true love. To know that my dad's heart belonged to Jaya and her mom made me resentful. I hated that bitch Jaya for having my dad's heart and stealing Isaiah from me.

Jayson did a lot for me, yeah, out of guilt though. But he loved him some Jaya. And the only reason why he had been tripping lately was because Jaya was acting like a bitch. Well shit was about to change. I was now the favorite daughter. And I was going to get everything I wanted for change. Jaya didn't know who she was fucking with.

"Talk to me." My father sat down across from me.

"I told Isaiah Jaya was my sister."

"What did he say?"

"He doesn't care. Daddy, he doesn't care about me or our baby." I whined.

"I told you. You can't make man a love you. I don't even know why you got pregnant on purpose." My father declared.

"And what about Jaya?"

"What about her?"

"The only reason Isaiah is with her is because she's pregnant."

"She's pregnant by another man. And he don't care because he loves her. You must accept that. But I told you to not get so wrapped up in this."

"But you're the one that made sure to put me in his path." I said low like anybody in this visiting room gave a fuck about what I was saying.

"Only to see why he had cut me off. But you fucked that up.

All I told you to do was see what was going on. You turned it into some dating shit. Now look at the situation. You and your sister in love with the same man."

"She's not my sister." I gritted my teeth.

"Well DNA says different. Instead of being mad at her, be mad at that punk ass nigga." My dad stated.

I rolled my eyes. "So what am I supposed to do now?"

"Just stick with the plan. Make sure Bando gets his cut."

"But...

"Just stick to the plan, Trinity." My father reiterated.

"Okay." I relented.

"Have you talked to Gio?"

"No, I been calling. He hasn't been answering."

"Is it going straight to voicemail?"

"Yeah?" I was not following what was going on.

"Fuck! I know they killed him. They probably think I'm involved. But I need you to see what Ice is saying."

"Dad, he changed his number on me. I don't even know where he lives now." I was feeling some type of way because my baby's father was ghosting me for a bitch that wasn't pregnant by him.

"Alright. I will look into it. Just stay away from Jaya, okay?"

"But she's playing house with my man."

"Baby, listen. You grew up in the suburbs, and where you lived people were okay with confrontation. But I advise you to not confront Jaya. She will fuck yo ass up."

I rolled my eyes but didn't say anything.

"Just stick to the plan, okay? Stay away from Jaya. I got this handled."

"But what about Isaiah?"

"That's up to you. What do you want to happen?"

"I want us to be a family with our baby." I stated.

"You can't make him be with you." My dad looked at me strangely.

Who says I can't?

❦

"Hi Auntie Key!" I went to hug my father's sister as soon as she opened her front door.

Keyonna stepped back with disgust written on her face. "Uh can I help you?" Keyonna stepped back.

"It's me Trinity..."

"I know who you are. But I don't know if you is my niece. I ain't never heard of you until my son said you was Jayson's daughter."

"I'm his daughter." I began as Keyonna stepped outside and closed her door behind her. I was a little taken back by how my own aunt didn't even invite me into her home. "The relationship with my mother and father is...complicated. He's..."

"My show is on. Girl, get to the point."

I swallowed hard. "I just wanted to build a relationship with you and JaShawn. Get to know my father's side of the family."

"Listen here little girl." Keyonna put her hand on her hip. "I still haven't heard shit from Jayson about you being our peoples. How old is you?"

"I'm twenty-seven." I replied.

"And you out here acting like that?"

"Excuse me?"

"Childish! You are running behind some nigga that obviously don't want you. Who still having a nigga's baby? Then you come to my *niece's* gender reveal on some Tyler Perry movie bullshit. Now, Jaya is mine. I made sure Jayson got a DNA on her. She is ours. You? I don't know. And even if you are, I don't like you. You messy. And now that I'm getting a good look at you, something ain't right with you. You have a blessed day." Keyonna crossed her arms.

I didn't know what to say. So I said nothing and walked back to my car. I wasn't understanding why I was being treated like the side bitch's baby when that title belonged to Jaya.

I fucking hated that bitch. She had the life and man I

wanted. The Mitchell family was my family. Isaiah was my baby daddy. Jayson was my dad. My mother was married to him. His name is on my birth certificate. I wasn't understanding why I was kept in the dark from my dad's family all these years. I needed answers and I needed them now.

As I drove south the condition of the city began to change from distressed to beautiful and Keyonna had the audacity to give me a hard time when her ass lived in the ghetto. I was tired of these uneducated, American car driving, food stamp using, low class, bitches. My purse alone probably cost more than Keyonna's whole house. She was just mad that I was better than Jaya. They all were.

"Mommy!" I called out as I walked into my mother's two-story apartment in Sunny Isles.

"I'm in the library." My mom shouted.

"Hello mother." I smiled as I sat down.

"Hello, darling." My mom looked up from her book. Kimberly was so pretty, and I just knew that I was going to be just as gorgeous when I hit my forties like my mom. She was the epitome of black don't crack.

"Mom," I got to it. "Why was we kept a secret? You were married to my dad. But somehow I'm treated like the side chick's baby."

"Did you try to go see Keyonna?"

"Yeah." I diverted my eyes.

"I see. Didn't go so well?"

"No."

"I'm sorry that this happened. The entire situation is complicated. I didn't set out for this to happen, Trinity. But don't get caught up in the drama. Even sitting in a prison cell Jayson is doing too much."

"But that's my dad." I could see why my mom wanted me to stay away from my dad's family but not my father.

"He's toxic and dangerous. He didn't keep you away, I did." My mother put her book down. "Our marriage was business to

begin with. He only got married to me because he got me preg-
nant and my dad wasn't having that. He was cheater and a liar.
Your grandpa's body wasn't even cold before Jayson divorced me.
Everybody around him ends up dying. The people that killed
Maya were trying to kill your dad. That bullet was meant for
Jayson. I just don't want you to be caught up in his bullshit."

I didn't know how to feel about what my mother just
told me.

"I know you love your dad. But he decided on revenge for his
side bitch. Maya was a nobody and he risked it all for her. That's
why he's in prison. He didn't care that his actions would stop
him from being in your life. He only cares about himself."

"No, he doesn't!" I felt the tears coming. "He loves me."

My mother stood over me and held my chin in her soft hand.
"Don't be blinded by the smoking mirrors, darling. What are you
going to do about this baby?"

"Me and Isaiah are trying to make it work for the baby."

"The man that you haven't brought around. That man?" My
mom stared into my teary eyes.

"He's very busy." I pulled away.

"I may have been born at night, but I wasn't born last night.
You keep telling me this story of this man you love. But I'm not
seeing any actions. Its looking like he doesn't want anything to
do with you or this baby. Don't let history repeat itself. I was
chasing after your dad. I even had my father make him marry
me. I thought having his first child would make him love me.
And you see how that went."

"I got to go." I stood to leave.

I was going show everybody. Come hell or high-water, Isaiah
and I was going to be together.

5

KEISHA

THREE MONTHS LATER

"Wow." Jaya wrapped her arms around me as I stood on her porch. "I missed you so much."

"I missed you too. I just been going through it."

"I knew it! I told Shawnie something wasn't right." Jaya replied as she let me into her house.

"It don't even matter. He shitted on me once again." I was never the bitch to chase a nigga. Shawnie knew the truth and he still said fuck me. So I was moving on. I wasn't about to let him or Tommy run me out of my city. I was here to stay.

"I'm sorry. He told me what happened with Tommy." Jaya did some weird waddle to sit on the couch. "Niggas are grimy."

"It looks like you swallowed a big ass basketball." I giggled as I changed the subject.

"Girl, I'm due any day. I stay hot, horny, and hungry. I'm over this shit."

"So, Ice got a baby on the way?" I recalled our conversation the other day.

Jaya blew out a long breath. "This bitch is due any day too.

We don't know if he's the daddy. He's going to do a DNA. I be trying not to think about it. The shit got me hot. But I can't be mad at nobody but me. Ice was with her. And here come my hot ass...

"Don't do that. Girl you and Ice are meant to be together. I been knowing that forever. At least he realizes that. You see Shawnie? He don't want me..." I wasn't trying not to cry but the tears fell.

I would have never gotten with Tommy if Shawnie wasn't entertaining bitches. I ran to the first nigga that said hello. I was so hurt. And now I lost the only man I loved. We lost our virginity together and it seemed like all our history don't mean shit to Shawnie.

"Aww," Jaya got up to wrap her arms around me. "Keisha don't cry."

"Baby" Both me and Jaya looked up to see Ice and Shawnie walking into the door. I quickly wiped my tears.

"You good?" Shawnie walked over to me.

"Don't say shit to me JaShawn." I stood. "Jaya, I forgot I had a nail appointment. I'll call you later." I lied.

I didn't give Jaya a chance to reply as darted to the door. I was barely out the door before Shawnie was grabbing me by the arm. "We need to talk."

"We don't need to talk about shit! Talk with your bitch." I snatched my arm away.

"The only reason you are tripping is because you picked the opps. I promise if shit was still good you wouldn't be worried about me. Don't be mad that you tried to play me but you ended up getting played."

"Fuck you bitch!" I was more hurt than everything. I didn't care how good shit was with Tommy, I knew that I was always going to gravitate back to Shawnie. "You punk ass... My sentence was cut short as Shawnie's lips crashed against mine. Every tension in my body was taken away. I needed this so much. But I had to realize that I wasn't built to be the side bitch. "Go back to your fiancé, Shawnie." I broke our kiss.

"Can I see you again? Take you to get some food or something?" Shawnie questioned.

I twisted my face up into a mug. "Why? Remember, I played myself." I tried to bypass Shawnie, but he stopped me a second time.

"You act like I ain't hurt too! You left me. I didn't leave you. I had no choice but to move on. I was out for six months and you didn't even try to reach out to me. Jaya is back for ten minutes and y'all kicking it. Then I get a bitch and now you want me back. The fuck?"

"Jaya popped up at my door. I didn't come around because I knew there was going to be a problem. But I finally chanced it because I wanted to see you. No matter how hard I tried to stay away, I couldn't. But let me tell you why the shit is dead between us. I was crying out for help and you thought it was some kid games type shit. You never questioned why I was acting different."

"Because that's the shit you did when I was in prison. The fuck! One day shit was good, the next, you fuckin' my boy."

"That's not what happened and I'm tired of trying to explain myself. You don't give a fuck about me and I accept that."

"I don't give a fuck about you? I fuckin' love you, Keisha. You're always on my mind. Dejah cooks in diamond butter, she chill as fuck and she suck my dick like her life depends on it. But all that can't compare to what I feel for you."

"Bye Shawnie." I walked to my car. I didn't want to hear that shit. Because when I tried to slide that bitch, Shawnie was trying to save her. This nigga was professing his love for me in private, but in front of his bitch I needed to move around. Yeah, I know a fuck boy when I see one.

"So, you think you can disappear and think I'm about to wait on you?"

"Tommy, I needed to get my mind right." I rubbed my hands down Tommy's chest.

"From what?" Tommy stared at me.

"You nigga! You started tripping and doing me wrong." I had to calm myself down. "But I realized that I shouldn't have left."

"No, you shouldn't have." Tommy cupped my ass. "So, this is your place?" Tommy looked around my home.

"Yeah, for now." I smiled.

"Take that shit off." Tommy tugged at my shorts. "You know you want some of this good dick."

"Yesss daddy!" I grinned as I pulled Tommy to the bedroom. "Let me set the mood." I pushed play on my Beats pill and turned the volume as high as it could go. "Come here babe." I beckoned Tommy with my index finger.

"That's what I'm talking about." Tommy walked over to me. "You...

Shawnie came out the closet swinging, knocking Tommy unconscious.

"It took you long enough." I rolled my eyes at Shawnie as we both looked down at Tommy. "I thought I was going have to end up giving him some pussy."

"You been fuckin' this nigga?" Shawnie replied.

"Don't start." I warned.

My relationship with Shawnie was more complicated than Chinese arithmetic. We hated each other, we loved each other, but we were there for each other. If that makes sense. Tommy had wreaked havoc in our lives and if it wasn't for him, Shawnie and I would still have been together. So, it was only natural for us to come together to kill this nigga.

"So, what's the move?" Shawnie looked at me. "You want to just shoot him? Because I know this is yo nigga but he ain't leaving this muthafucka alive."

"Why you got to keep taking jabs at me like I don't know I

fucked up? I fucked the opps! Alright? Damn, quit rubbing salt into the wound, Shawnie. You act like I want this nigga to live. He raped me...

"He what?"

"When I was at your house that week. When I came back home, he raped me." My voice dropped because I was trying to not break down.

"Why the fuck you didn't tell me?" Shawnie got angry.

"I tried to but you wasn't returning none of my calls."

"Keisha I should fuck your ass up. You should have told me when you first called."

"You didn't care!" My emotions were flooding my whole body. I was so broken at the time and when Shawnie didn't react to how funny I was acting, I felt like he didn't care. But I just couldn't keep letting Tommy dictate how I lived. So that's why I came back to Miami. I was going to kill this nigga on my own, but Shawnie reached out to me and we decided to do this shit together.

"Shut the fuck up, Kesh." Shawnie snatched up Tommy.

Shawnie began to bitch slap Tommy like he was a hoe that been on the corner all night and didn't make no money. Tommy woke up groggy and Shawnie began to flip out.

"Nigga you raped my girl?" Shawnie yelled. "Go get the butcher knife, Kesh!" Shawnie began to tie up Tommy with the rope he had in his back pocket. I tossed Shawnie the duct tape and he taped up Tommy's mouth. Tommy tried to fight off Shawnie, but Shawnie was a big ass nigga. The whole scene looked like a toddler trying to fight a giant. Tommy didn't stand a chance.

All I wanted to do was do a simple kill of a bullet to the head. But this crazy muthafucka wanted to turn into an ID channel killer. "Bae, I just got this apartment. I still got to live here." I tried to calm Shawnie down. "Can we stick to the plan? We just put him in the trunk, take him to the Everglades, shoot him and leave him."

"That was before I found out he raped you." Shawnie stepped over a tied-up Tommy and got into my space. "When your mama's boyfriend tried to rape you, what I do? I killed that nigga. Ain't shit changed. Baby, I don't give a fuck what we got going on. I got a whole bitch, but you always going to have my heart. And because of that, the nigga going to die...slowly."

"Ok. But can you torture him somewhere else? I don't want that blood all in my carpet." I tried to reason with Shawnie.

"Bet." Shawnie quickly pecked my lips.

"Don't kiss me. We still ain't good nigga!" I stepped back.

"But you calling me bae?" Shawnie smirked kissing me a second time.

"What the fuck ever. Keep that same energy in front of your bitch."

"Alright, bet." Shawnie lifted Tommy like a bag of potatoes. "You drive." Shawnie said over his shoulder.

It took an hour to get to the Everglades and Shawnie was acting like we were on a date. I ain't going to lie, my feelings for him were still there. But I refused to be the side chick. And I refused to sit around and wait for this nigga to decide if he wanted me or Dejah.

"I know you want to torture him and I somewhat do too. But I just ain't got the stomach for limbs displaced and shit." I told Shawnie as we got out of the car.

Darkness had fell over the Everglades, waking the predators who was looking for their next meal. Which was evident by the strange animal noises coming from the bush. I didn't want to be out here any longer than I had to. Plus, I was a killer not a serial killer. I killed out necessity, not for fun.

"So just a bullet to the head?" Shawnie questioned as he popped the trunk.

"Please."

"Whatever you want, Kesh." Shawnie dragged a screaming Tommy out of the trunk. But his screams were muffled from the duct tape.

As soon as Tommy hit the ground I shot him in the leg. Tommy yelped out in pain as Shawnie looked at me with admiration. "You better stop. You getting my dick hard. You know I like it when you get thuggish."

"Shut the fuck up." I rolled my eyes, but I had a grin on my face. I was timid my whole life and then Shawnie showed me something different and I ain't looked back since.

"Do you, ma." Shawnie got in my space and kissed my cheek. "Kill him."

I side eye Shawnie as I bit down on my lip. It pissed me off the way he flooded my essence. It was like when God created me, he said, *"I'ma make this one for Shawnie."*

I didn't speak as I shot Tommy two more times. One in the groin and then in the head. It was lights out for his bitch ass.

"You feel better?" Shawnie asked as he lowered the gun in my hands as my tears fell. My mind was flooded by being treated like a pawn in Tommy's beef with Shawnie. Tommy sought me out and I fell for his lies. I shitted on the man that loved me for a nigga that degraded, hit, and raped me. I was on some stupid bitch shit.

"I don't know." I shrugged.

"Listen. Stay with me for the night. Not on no smashing shit either. Since that's what you think that's all I want. I'm talkin' on some relaxation shit. *Love and Basketball* is on Amazon Prime. We can grab some Miami Heat burgers from LoKal's, eat popcorn, drink 1800, and play dominos." Shawnie named all my favorites.

"And what about your bitch?"

"What about her?"

I blew out some air as Shawnie began to drive. "Typical Shawnie shit."

"If nothing else you going to always be my best friend. But I just can't bring myself to do the bitch that been down for me wrong. Do I wish that this shit with Tommy never happened? Hell yeah. Do I wish that I proposed to you rather than her?

Fuck yeah. And the fact that no matter how good of a woman Dejah is I can't seem to stay away from you. I'm like a crackhead looking for dope. You can't keep me away. But I got to do what is right. You know how I am about loyalty. I can't hurt that girl like you hurt me Kesh."

"Wow! I built your ass into this good faithful man and she reaps the benefits! I been wanting you since I was in kindergarten nigga. Kindergarten! Loyalty? How I did you? I been down for you since the sandbox! Who was taking penitentiary chances for your ass? Huh? You put me on to selling drugs and shooting muthafuckas. When you jumped off the porch, I was right there with you. We were Bonnie and Clyde before there was a Bonnie and Clyde. I'm telling you to come home but you want me on the side and I love myself too much to be your side bitch."

"I'm not asking you to be my side bitch, Kesh. I'm asking you to be my friend. Everything you said is true. I'm not shit without you. Just like I molded you. You molded me. But when you found out that Tommy was my boy why did you still fuck with him? When the nigga threatened you, why didn't you tell me? Instead, you were playing mind games. I'm a nigga, I don't be doin' that read between the lines shit. You got to tell me. But you been knowing that."

"Because you were entertaining bitches. I couldn't say shit because I was scared that he was going to kill you! Even then I tried to tell you. I said, 'Wait for me. I got us. I'm going to fix it.' And what did you do? Go ask the next bitch to marry you." I threw up my hands in defeat.

"I don't want to go back and forth." Shawnie released the anger he had. "I did some foul shit. You did some foul shit. I want you in my life...as my friend."

"We lost our virginity together. You are my first everything. Including the first man who ever gave a fuck about me. Excuse me. Out of Jaya, yo mama, and my grandma, the first person to give a fuck about me! I'm the only one who knows your secrets, flaws, insecurities, and failures, and vice versa. We got a bond that defines time and reason and you want to put me in the friend zone?" I snickered because after everything, Shawnie wanted to be my friend.

That shit was worse than being a side bitch. I know there is the saying that *if you love someone you would want them happy, even if it's not with you.* And that was some straight bullshit. I only wanted him. I stayed with Tommy because I was hurt. I'm a bad ass chocolate bitch. Niggas wanted me like a PPP loan. And yet I only wanted JaShawn Mitchell. Either Shawnie and I was going to be together or kick rocks nigga.

"What do you want me to do about Dejah, Kesh? That girl ain't did shit wrong. You just want me to break up with her?"

"Yes nigga! Or leave me the fuck alone."

"So, I guess some pussy is out of the question?" Shawnie looked over at me.

"You a trifling ass nigga." I mushed Shawnie.

"But you love it." Shawnie rubbed his hand between my thighs.

My pussy and my heart were on the same page as I let out a soft moan.

I hated that he was right.

I did love his rude, trifling ass.

✥ 6 ✥
ICE

"**I** see you knocking down everything moving." My OG prodded and all I could do was put my head in my hands. "Do I have a grand baby on the way? Who is the baby mama? Because I'm confused."

"Ma, I told you that Jaya's baby is mine but not biologically. As far as Trinity, I don't know. I smashed only three times."

"Well, that girl came to my house...

"Who? Trinity?" I just knew it was her ass.

"Yeah. She said that y'all was together for six months and you started cheating on her with Jaya. And the reason you ain't Jaya's baby's daddy is because she was cheating on her husband with you."

"The bitch lying." I raised up my head. "I was fucking with her for a month. Jaya's husband was cheating on Jaya with her friend. She's pregnant and came back home. We started messing around and I broke up with Trinity. I just didn't know how to tell you that Jaya's baby wasn't mine."

"And they are sisters? This is some Jerry Springer shit." My OG passed me the blunt and I needed to smoke because my nerves were shot.

"Shit is all bad."

"What are you going do if this is your baby, Isaiah?"

"I'ma take care of my son. I just don't want to deal with Trinity."

"What I tell you about raw dicking these bitches?"

"That's the thing. I stay strapped, especially with her. The pussy was trash. That's why I hit it only three times!" I looked at my OG as she sat next to me on the couch. My mom was more like my friend than my mother. It wasn't always like that, but as I got older the more we was able to be friends. Because when I was younger, Tia wasn't playing no games. I was a child and I stayed in a child's place.

"And Jaya?"

"That may not be my blood running through that little girl but that is my daughter. Me and Jaya trying to work it out. She mad, shit I am too. But we going to stay together."

"If that's your baby then that's my granddaughter. Son, I was younger than you doin' dumb shit. I was with this nigga and got pregnant by your daddy. My ex was pissed. But shit I was seventeen. I didn't know what the fuck I was doing. After your dad died, I tried to work shit out with my ex. Which was a big mistake. The nigga was crazy. I barely got away. Live your life son. But just keep in mind that if this baby is yours, Trinity ain't going to let you be happy without her. Keep your guard up. And I'm not trying to be mean but if you got to kill the bitch, then you are going have to kill the bitch."

I looked at my mother strangely. She was basically saying if Trinity got out of hand for me to kill her. I didn't like Trinity, but I wasn't going to take her away from her child that might be my child too.

"What?" My mom shot me a look.

"You crazy."

"But I'm right though."

"Ma, can I have some money" Isis walked in the door followed by Indica. "Hey Isaiah." My sisters greeted me.

I was making more of an effort to help my OG with my

sisters, and looking at my sisters' appearance, shit was getting better. They weren't wearing the Cora dresses, but they weren't dressed like city girls either.

I gave a head nod.

"Ma, can I have some money for the church carnival." Isis asked.

"Church?" I shockingly questioned. Damn my sister was a different person.

"Them church girls is busted. So when me and Indica slide through all them niggas be checking for us. Brother Jackson just gave me $100 to get my nails done." Isis stuck her tongue out as her and Indica high fived.

I stood corrected. Isis went from a regular hoe to a church hoe.

"You're fucking these old deacons to get your nails done?" I was reaching for my belt.

"Mama! Tell Isaiah that I'm still a virgin. And Brother Jackson is only eighteen, dummy."

I looked at my mother. "Is that true?"

"Yeah. I took them to the doctor last week. They some virgins."

"So, you just pretend to be fast? Let me tell you from a nigga's perspective. If it walks like a duck, talks like a duck, it's a duck. Meaning if you dress like a hoe, act like a hoe, niggas is going to treat you and try to fuck you like a hoe."

"Well, we go to church for the Lord and the niggas. But I'm only talking to Davion, aka Brother Jackson. He respects the fact that I ain't smashing." Isis rolled her eyes.

"But just a few months ago you had R. Kelly up in mama's house, and Indica's bad ass stole my weed."

"You always think the worse of us, but you out here fuckin' sisters. Nigga bye." Indica spoke up.

"You told them?" I turned to my mom.

"Was it supposed to be a secret?"

"So, who is really the hoe?" Indica smirked.

"Ma get your daughters." I got mad.

"Leave your brother alone. He didn't know they was sisters."

"Ma, he started coming for...

"Aht aht. Don't y'all start that bullshit. I pick peace today." My OG got up from the couch. "I'm about to go take me a nap and then brick up this dope. I got a long night and I want some peace and quiet."

"Alright ma. I'ma head out. I left them bands for you in the safe." I stood up and kissed my mother's cheek.

"It better be all the money too. This ain't no consignment store." My mom replied. "I'll have Carlise drop of the bricks to the trap."

"Alright." I walked to the front door. "I'm about to get in these streets."

"Take heed to what I said, son. I don't trust that damn Trinity. While I would love to have a grandson, I don't want you to have deal with some crazy bitch to see your son."

"Facts. I don't know what Jayson going to do next, ma." My mom had told me to fall back. But I needed to have shit resolved.

"I told you. I got you. Mama going to take care of it. I got shit in the works. Just be patient baby boy."

⚜

ONE MONTH LATER

I didn't think I could love someone like I loved my little girl and it didn't even matter that I wasn't the bio daddy. Jaya and I was in love with some Israel. She was such a good baby, considering she was always in someone's arms. At three weeks, Israel looked just like Jaya. Our little girl was absolutely gorgeous.

I been at the trap all night and now I was chilling with my girl and my daughter laying on my chest as I tried to keep my eyes open, but I was losing the battle.

"Your baby mama is at the door." I heard Jaya say in my sleep. I looked up and saw Trinity holding a one-month-old Isaiah Jr. Not only was the fucking baby mine but she named him after me. I wanted to slit my own damn wrists when them papers came in the mail saying I was the father. I wore a condom and now I was stuck with this bitch for life. I loved my son, but this was some bullshit.

"I told you about that pop-up shit." I stood up with Israel in my arms.

"Izzy wanted to see his daddy." Trinity adjusted the baby on her shoulder.

"Bitch you wanted to come over here. Don't pop up at my muthafuckin house!" Jaya got angry.

"This ain't your house. This is Isaiah's, *sis.*" Trinity smirked and there was so much shit behind Trinity calling Jaya sis.

"Bitch I don't give a fuck about you being my sister. And this is me and Isaiah's house. You better be glad you're holding that baby."

"You mean your nephew?" Trinity taunted.

"Baby," I intervened as I got in between Jaya and Trinity. "Let me handle this."

"No! This hoe popping up at my fucking house with her keep a nigga baby on some sneaky shit. I ain't got nothing against the baby. I don't mind him being over here. I know that's your son. It's that bitch!" Jaya pointed over my shoulder. "That's who I have a problem with."

"You really about to trip with your blood sister behind a nigga?" Trinity said from behind me, flaming the fire with bullshit.

"Shut the fuck up!" I turned to Trinity. "Don't come to my house disrespecting my girl. You are just the baby mama. That's it. And that shit was on accident. Don't pop up at my house, Trinity. If my son needs something, call me. He's one month old. All he wants to do is eat, shit, and cry. I'm telling you now. Using my son to get at me ain't going to work. I don't want you." I got in Trinity's face as I held my daughter.

Trinity was not bothered by what I said as she smiled and mouthed the words. "I love you too."

I stepped back because this bitch was crazy. It would be a cold day in hell before I entertained Trinity's bitch ass.

"Give me my baby." Jaya reached for Israel as she began to cry. "I'm going to feed Israel. You do what you need to do. But get this hoe out of my house."

"Okay." I grabbed Jaya by the chin and kissed her. Hopefully letting Trinity know that nothing would ever transpire between us. Even though I wasn't getting no pussy because Jaya said she was still healing, but how long does it take for some pussy to snap back. A nigga was so horny that when Jaya was making macaroni and cheese the other day my dick got hard. Even though I wasn't getting none, I rather jack off with sandpaper than cheat on my bitch with Trinity. These last three weeks was about to be hard as fuck. However, Jaya was making it work with them oral skills.

"So, you leaving Izzy or what?" I got to the point.

"I was thinking we could go somewhere and talk about a parenting plan...

"We can talk right here."

"Well first. My mom is throwing me a post-natal baby shower. I think it's important that we are presented as united unit."

"What the fuck are you saying?" I hated when Trinity used fancy words, bitch get to the point.

"I want you at the baby shower, Isaiah."

"What I need to go for? Quit trying to make this shit into more than what it is."

"What about our son? He needs to see his daddy loving his mommy."

"When you play stupid games, you get stupid prizes. You shouldn't expect love from a nigga that you trapped."

"I didn't trap you!"

"What you call it then? I used a condom the three times we fucked. I broke up with you. And here you come hollering I'm the daddy. If it wasn't for them papers, I wouldn't be speaking to you. So, are you going to leave the baby or not?"

"No! I don't trust your bitch. She might abuse my baby."

"He's been coming over. Jaya ain't did shit to Izzy. She only wants to whoop your ass. And the only reason she hasn't is because I asked her not to. This back-and-forth shit is stupid. You leaving my son or not?"

"No."

"Bet." I opened the front door so that Trinity could leave. I love my son but if Trinity thought she was about to be holding him over my head, she had me fucked up. Izzy been in this world for only four weeks and this bitch was already wilding. This was the fifth time she had popped up at my house in the last eight days. Fuck this shit, I wasn't about to be playing bitter baby mama games. I know it was Jayson's punk ass that gave Trinity the addy in the first place because Jaya used to write him. But as far as I know, she wasn't fucking with him anymore. Trinity had a rude awaken coming her way, she should be getting served with a court ordered parenting plan any day now. All this popping up shit was about to stop, because in the parenting plan it says we will meet in a public place for pick up and drop offs. And on top of that, Jaya and I was moving in few days. We both wanted something bigger and a new beginning. I was keeping the town-house. But as far as where me and Jaya was laying our heads, we were moving to a house. So Trinity could pop up all she wanted, nobody was going to be here.

"So you don't want to see your son?" Trinity continued with the mind games.

"I'm not about to play these games..."

"Isaiah, I'm telling you now. Either you get with the program or you will never see your son again."

"What program?" This bitch was so weird.

"Us being together for our child. It's not fair to Izzy and I want our son to be in a loving two parent home."

"Well, you should have gotten pregnant by a nigga that loved you. Don't threaten me with my son. It won't end well for you."

"Fine. If that's how you want to play, Isaiah. You think you and your little whore going to play house? You will be hearing from my father. He already doesn't like you..."

"Bitch," My voice raised because I was hot. I didn't like muthafuckas thinking I was scared of the next man. "What the fuck Jayson going to do? Bitch ain't nobody scared of your punk ass daddy or you. Tell that nigga to holla at me. As a matter fact, tell him to add me back on his visiting list. I'll tell him my damn self. I'll be there next Saturday!"

My mom's words were taking residence in my head.

Trinity ain't going to let you be happy without her. Keep your guard up. And I'm not trying to be mean but if you got to kill the bitch. You are going have to kill the bitch. Period!

I hated that my mom was right. I just might have to kill the mother of my son.

❦ 7 ❦

DEJAH

"**B**itch, tell my baby to her face she ain't eating this month!" I watched Shanice yell at the receptionist lady here at the food stamp office.

Shanice was having some car trouble so I volunteered to take her to the food stamp office since they cut her stamps off. I didn't know she was going to be up in here acting a fool. But Shanice was wild so I guess I should not have been too surprised.

"Ma'am please calm down..."

"How am I going to be calm and you muthafuckas playing with my livelihood? I want to speak with my social worker. Heffa going to run me my stamps." Shanice crossed her arms.

"Can I have your name?" The receptionist replied calmly. I worked in customer service and there was no way that I would have been this calm. She better than me because I would have been called security.

"Shanice Anderson."

The receptionist began to type. "It looks like due to your new income your monthly food stamps will be seventeen dollars..."

"Seventeen dollars? I need to talk to Lashauna. Cause uh uh,

38

this ain't it. I got four kids and you muthafuckas want to punish me for not being a lazy bitch? Tell her to come up here."

"Lashauna is out for the day. But I can send her a message via email."

"Whatever. Tell her. You ready?" The receptionist shook her head up and down. "Quit playing with me. You know damn well I need them stamps. You ain't got to call, just run me my stamps. That's it. You have a good day." Shanice walked off.

"What the hell is wrong with you?" I asked Shanice as she walked up on me. "You make enough money to buy food."

"And? I need all my coins." Shanice replied as we walked out the food stamp building. "What's the move? My mama got the kids so, I'm outside!" Shanice twerked.

I couldn't do nothing but laugh. One thing about Shanice, she was going to make shit happen. She may have been ghetto, but she was about her money and her kids. I have never seen her kids or her house dirty, and just because she had four kids by four different daddies didn't mean that she was a hoe. She wasn't havin' niggas running in and out her house. And she certainly wasn't paying for dick. She was just a pretty brown chick that didn't put up with the bullshit. She was more than my best friend; she was like my sister. I fucked with her and her bad ass kids.

"You hungry?"

"Wait, don't Lil' Way work at the food truck with Shawnie?" Shanice smiled.

"Yeah, he do."

"Who he live with? How many kids he got? He do powder?"

"He lives by himself. He has two daughters. And he doesn't do cocaine."

"He still fucking with the baby mama?"

"I don't think so. But I don't know for sure." I spoke honestly.

"I'ma find out. Let's go to the food truck then."

The line for the Miami Hustle food truck was down the

block. I was so happy for my baby as he pursued his dream. I been here since the beginning and to see this food truck so successful was everything. Business was booming and Shawnie added a second truck that drove to businesses. I even put the word out at my job.

Everybody at Dish loved the food and it gave me a chance to see my baby. The only downside was that I had to check a few bitches about stepping to my man. But Shawnie didn't entertain them hoes. The only bitch that had me questioning Shawnie's fidelity was Keisha's ass.

"Hey babe." Shawnie kissed my lips as Shanice and I approached the food truck. This was my man's shit, and I made a beeline to the side of truck; bypassing the long line.

"Hi. Where's Lil' Way?" I questioned as looked around.

Shawnie snatched me up. "I know your ass ain't asking me about another nigga?"

I forgot that Shawnie was sensitive about his girl and his boys interacting. "Not for me! For Shanice." I pointed behind me.

"Yeah, ok. Don't get you and that nigga fucked up."

"I'm faithful, nigga. Are you?"

Shawnie didn't look my way. "I got to tell you something, Dejah."

I felt it in my heart before Shawnie said a damn thing. Shawnie grabbed me by the hand and led me to behind the truck.

"You fucked Keisha?" I could feel my heart beating faster by the second.

"You know I love you, Dejahnae. I..."

"Whatever nigga! Did you fuck Keisha?" Because love should have kept his dick in his pants.

"I almost did."

"What the fuck is almost?"

"I wanted to. Shit I kissed her. I touched her. But I didn't smash."

"But you wanted to? What stopped you?"

"I couldn't do you wrong, bae. I got to go with the one who hasn't changed. The loyal one. The faithful one."

"So, I'm the consolation prize? The less difficult one. The safe choice. I'm done. It's obvious I'm in the way of you and Keisha being able to be together." I took off my engagement ring and put in Shawnie's hand. "Here. Give it to that bitch. And since we are being honest, I had abortion five months ago. I didn't know if you or another nigga was the daddy." I tried to drop that last bomb and walk away but Shawnie grabbed me by my jugular.

"You killed my baby, bitch?"

I think I peed a little bit, I was so scared. Shawnie was a big ass nigga with an even bigger temper. "It ain't no fun when the rabbit got the gun. Is it?" I smirked as I tried to hide my fear. I wanted Shawnie to hurt as much as I did.

"You're cheating on me?" Shawnie got in my face.

"Just like you! If you're cheating, I'm cheating junior."

"You a rat ass bitch!" Shawnie yelled as he let me go. "And to think that I was going to marry your ass. I cut off all these bitches for you, Zo."

"Yeah, everybody but Keisha! I lied. I was only fucking you, but I was pregnant. But I lost the baby. Like I said I'm done! Go be for everybody like you been doing. I'm too good of a woman to be playing second choice to some bitch ass felon!" I screamed. To say my heart was broken was an understatement.

I didn't even know I was pregnant. I'm thinking I'm having a bad period and my doctor said that I had a miscarriage and wanted to perform a D&C. I didn't tell Shawnie because why bring him unnecessary pain. I was on the pill, but I had my doctor put me on the IUD to avoid another slip up.

"I told you I wanted to smash and I didn't! Why the fuck you ain't tell me you was pregnant, Dejah? A nigga be honest and now you want to..."

"Fuck you nigga!" I tried to walk away but Shawnie snatched me up a second time. "Let me go! I'm done with you!" I cried.

"Baby stop!" Shawnie put me in a bear hug. I was crying and usually shit like this had me ready to forgive but not this time.

Shawnie tried to kiss me and I let him. As soon as he thought shit was good, I made my way to my car.

If I let this shit slide that meant that I would always be in his eyes...Dejah the stupid bitch. Lord knows I love Shawnie. But I got to love me more.

⚜

"Bitch, you better be glad I love you." Shanice rolled her eyes as she stood at my desk. "I looked up and your ass was gone. What the hell happened?"

"We broke up. It's over." I stated.

"I'm sorry friend. These niggas ain't shit."

"Don't I know." I thought of Shawnie and how he was such a fuck boy. I wasted all this time on a man that used me. "I'm about to head out of here." I began to gather up my things. "You good?"

"I'm driving Lil' Way's whip. He don't have to work today. So he at the house..."

"Huh? Girl it's only been nine days. How..."

"Aht aht, don't ask. You up and left me then...boom! I'm fucking with the fuck boy's bestie. Girl, I can't explain it my damn self. I got four kids, do I look like I got time to be playing games? I don't even know how to date. Ten minutes in, I be ready to suck some dick and calling the nigga bae."

"Bye!" I laughed as I put my purse over shoulder.

"Call me."

I rolled my eyes with a smile and headed to the door.

When we fight, can't let the world know
Don't tell the group chat or let your girls know
They be happy to see you down
They be happy to see you down

And my heart cold, but you heat it up
Get you to the crib naked, beat it up

The Lil' Durk ballad blasted from Shawnie's 2020 Yukon Denali. He had two niggas that worked at Dish holding two big ass flower arrangements. They didn't even know him. But Shawnie was so damn intimidating that he probably told them to hold the flowers.

Want you to be my girl, no friendship
I gave her the code to the mansion
Want me to suck her toes, she demand it
Oh, ice out her pendant
Put a Rollie on her left wrist

Shawnie rapped as he opened a box revealing a beautiful Rolex. I'm not going to lie I had a few tears. "Love you" by Lil' Durk was our song. I made eye contact with Shawnie and kept it moving to my car.

I didn't get far as Shawnie stopped me. "I know you see me, Dejah."

"What do you want?" I snatched my arm away.

"You got me out here like a fiend. I can't sleep. I can't eat. I feel..."

"Go tell Keisha then." I tried to walk off.

"I killed Tommy. Me and Keisha. That's why I was around her. I let my emotions get the best of me..."

"That's fine. Continue to let your emotions rule you. Because it's obvious that's where you want to be."

"I see now that I was playing games. With her. With you. And that shit ain't fair to either one of y'all. That's some bitch nigga shit. But in these last nine days. I did some soul searching and I choose you bae."

I broke down laughing. I know this nigga wasn't serious. "Miss me with that bullshit. What the fuck I look like? I ain't

43

sitting around waiting for your bitch ass. You had your chance, JaShawn. Go be with the bitch that fucks on your homeboys. You ain't man enough to be with a woman like me."

Shawnie looked around as he shook his head up and down knowingly. Before I knew it, I was being hoisted up in the air and being put over Shawnie's shoulder. "Put me down!" I yelled. "Help I'm being kidnapped!"

"Dejah is everything okay?" The security guard walked up on us in the parking lot.

I didn't see what was going on, but I heard the gun being cocked back before Shawnie placed me on my feet. "Nigga mind your fucking business. Me and my bitch having a domestic. Dejah tell this nigga you good." Shawnie looked over at me as he had his gun trained on the security guard.

I closed my eyes to remain calm before I spoke. This nigga was real life crazy. "I'm fine, Joe. We are leaving now."

The security guard looked uncertain about leaving but what the hell was he going to do? He had a flashlight and whistle and Shawnie had a .45 automatic.

"Nigga," Shawnie lunged forward like he was going to punch the security guard and Joe jumped; causing Shawnie to laugh. "Scary ass nigga. Fucking Topflight Security ass nigga. What the fuck you going to do? But get your ass kicked like your daddy used to." Shawnie turned to me like Joe had disappeared. "You getting in the car on your own or do I need to put you in there? Don't look at this Dae-Dae looking ass nigga. He ain't about to save you."

I crossed my left arm across my chest and palmed my head with my right hand. "What about my car?"

"Dejah's car good?" Shawnie looked at Joe.

"I-I-..."

"Nigga! Is her car good or not?"

"My shift is over in an hour. I can't be responsible for..."

"I'll call someone to pick it up. Come on!" Shawnie began to walk back to his car as I stood there with Joe.

"Dejahnae." Shawnie turned around. "You better bring your ass on. Ain't no breaking up. Damn I said I was sorry."

But I didn't take a step.

"You should go..." Joe found his voice and I just mugged him. *Bitch ass Topflight pussy ass nigga.*

"Don't make me come get you."

I rolled my eyes as I stomped towards Shawnie. Shawnie had a goofy ass smile on his face as he tried to touch me.

"Don't touch me!" I snatched away.

Shawnie had the two dudes that was holding the flowers put them in the backseat before he pulled off from the curb.

ONE HOUR LATER

I was clawing the sheets like Yvette from *Baby Boy* as Shawnie ate between my legs like he ain't ate in weeks. An orgasm as big as a tsunami had erupted throughout my body causing me to moan louder.

Soon as the aftershocks of nutting subdued, I was trying to leave.

"What the fuck, Dejah?" Shawnie looked at me crazy.

"It's over Shawnie! You ain't going to keep playing with my feelings."

"I know." Shawnie got on his knees. "I know I fucked up. But I don't want to lose you, Flower. I was real life sick without you. I was wrong!" Shawnie patted his chest with force. "Baby don't leave me."

"I'm done. How many bitches you fucked since I been dealing with you? How many bitches you entertained? And now you seeing that none of them bitches were solid and now you want to choose me? Nope! I'm good!"

"Ok. All you are saying is that I was a stupid ass nigga. And I'm saying that I know. *Can't no one fuck this up 'cause this too deep*

45

with us. But I love you, that's why I'm into you. My baby, oh, oh, that's why I'm into you. My wifey, yeah, yeah, that's why I'm into you. But I love you, but I love you!" Shawnie rapped as he kissed me on me.

I hated him.

"And what about Keisha?" I looked down at Shawnie.

"I told her that as much as I care about her. I loved you and my future is with you. She ain't got no choice but to respect it. You got the bond, the ring, and my heart." Shawnie pulled my engagement ring out of his pocket and slid it down my finger.

I didn't speak as Shawnie began to trail kisses from my lips to my collarbone causing me to shiver in anticipation. I bit down on my lip as Shawnie slowly spread my legs.

"You my forever bae?" Shawnie stared into my eyes. I was so full of emotions and all I could do was shake my head up and down.

"I'm not going make you regret it either." Shawnie laid me back on the bed slowly as he freed himself from his clothes. "That's on me."

Fifty percent of my problem was that Shawnie had that fire. I ain't never been fucked the way Shawnie dicked me down. Shawnie inhaled my moans as he entered into me slowly. Shawnie wasn't even in the pussy for long before he was maneuvering me to straddle him. The shit hurt so good as my juices flowed like melted ice down his shaft. Shawnie was gripping my thighs as he helped me bounce on his dick.

"Fuck." I let my head fall back as ecstasy swarmed around me and my nigga. Shawnie was so adventurous as he stood up and continued to pump into me. The only thing I had to hold on to was his neck as he dove deep and fast in my slippery opening.

"Shawnie!" I yelped out because I didn't think the dick could get better but Shawnie was proving me wrong by the second.

"You my forever bae?" Shawnie's voice deepened as he grunted in my ear.

I didn't have any words as another orgasm ripped through my body like a slasher film. My moans energized Shawnie as he pumped faster in me. My eyes rolled in the back of my head, and I was feeling like that bitch from the *Conjuring* as this nut possessed my whole body.

I was panting heavily as Shawnie nutted too as we collapsed onto his bed.

"You think you going to be fucking me like that and leave me? You got me fucked up!" Shawnie brought me into his arms. "Ain't no breaking up."

"Whatever." I grinned.

"We need to decide on a date for this wedding babe. I'm done playing games. When you told me about losing our baby, that shit hit me hard. I never thought about being a father. But I want that shit with you. So as soon as we say I do. I'm putting a baby in you."

I began to chuckle. "You don't have one romantic bone in your body!"

"I'm a hood nigga. If wasn't for Jaya I wouldn't know about no flowers. Shit, I thought eating some pussy, giving you some money, and tripping on a nigga was romantic."

I didn't even respond. Shawnie was a real-life street nigga. But he was my street nigga.

8

JAYA

"Happy Birthday, Jaya!" Everyone yelled with the DJ as soon as it hit midnight.

Ice wrapped his arms around me for a quick kiss on the cheek as the bottle girls flooded the VIP with bottles of Dusse`, Ace of spades, Grey Goose, 1942, 1800, Patron, Ciroc, and Hennessey XO, followed by a four tier Hennessy themed birthday cake that was adorned with mini Hennessy bottles, gold French macarons, and sparklers. The whole sight brought tears to my eyes because Shawnie, Dejah, and Ice really went out for my twenty-fourth birthday.

It had been over nine months since I had drink or hit a blunt, and I was overdue for some adult time. Israel was with Ice's family for the next week and I was going to be lit every fucking day.

"Make a wish Jay." Ice spoke as the cake came closer.

"I don't need to. I got everything I want." I smiled at my man as I blew out my candles.

"I don't know about that." Ice rubbed his hands together. The club went dark as the only light came from the sparklers and the large screen above the DJ booth. I was really praying

48

that another one of my dad's secret kids wasn't going to pop out to say she was Ice's new baby mama. I've been through hell ever since Trap Star said that he wanted to be with my best friend and kicked me out. The best thing that came from all the pain I endured was my daughter and Ice. I don't think I could mentally do another fucked up surprise.

The screen flashed pictures of me and Ice throughout the years. The glow up was real because we used to be busted. I mean I was always cute. But I was so damn skinny and had the chest of a twelve-year-old boy and a booty that was flat as a pancake. Ice was somewhat cute, but he had them thick ass glasses that let him see what was going on next week, pimples, and he was skinny as fuck.

"Y'all sho was ugly!" Shawnie mimicked Shug Avery and everybody busted out laughing.

"Fuck you!" I giggled.

The last picture was taken about a week ago and me and my man was looking good. The transformation was real.

I was so damn slow as I read the words on the screen. "Will you marry me?" I looked confused as I tried to figure out what was going on. I turned to Ice and he was on one knee holding an engagement ring.

Jay, you already know how I feel about you. I ain't got no long speech. We been rocking since we were some kids. You got my heart and my daughter. Will you marry me?"

"Yes!" I jumped into Ice's arms as everybody cheered.

"You know I don't play about this one." Shawnie slapped hands with Ice.

"Nigga I don't play about this one."

"Facts, bro. Congratulations!" Shawnie hugged me. "I'm proud of you sis. Do right by this nigga. He really do love you. It been killing me to keep this shit hush hush for a minute."

"You knew this whole time?" I asked Shawnie.

"Yeah."

"Congrats, girl!" Keisha came out of nowhere.

"Aww thank you best friend." I hugged Keisha. With my arms still around Keisha I seen some older man and a girl around our age. "Uh who is these people Harpo?"

"Oh. Let me introduce you to them." Keisha broke our hug. "This is Bernard." Keisha got into the older man's space as she focused on Shawnie and Dejah like I wasn't even there. "And this is his daughter, Sidney."

"Oh. Ok. Can I holler at you?" I didn't let Keisha respond as I snatched her ass in the corner. "Bitch why are you here with R. Kelly? What is going on?"

"Bernard?"

"Yes. Mr. Bernard."

"He's not that old, He's only forty-eight."

"What the fuck Keisha! He's old enough to be your daddy. You may as well have said eighty-eight. I know you are upset about you and Shawnie but sis...fucking Mr. Otis is not the way to go."

"I am not with *Bernard* because of Shawnie! I'm happy!"

"With a stepdaughter that is the same age as you? You ain't got to front with me. I know you. I'm not saying don't be happy but don't get with the first nigga all because you're hurt."

"Like you did?" Keisha put her hands on her hips. "Married and pregnant. Fucking the first nigga you see when you touched down to Miami."

"That is different." I was trying to suppress my anger. "You know how Ice and I feel about each other."

"But ain't he your sister's baby daddy?" Keisha through hell of shade.

"Look," My anger matched Keisha's. "It's obvious that you are mad about Shawnie but don't take that shit out on me. You fucked his homeboy not me."

"Fuck you, Jaya. You ain't my best friend anyway. How you got the opps here knowing she fuckin' my man."

"Kesh, that's not fair."

"Why not? Your loyalty is to Shawnie not me."

"That's my brother. That's family" I defended my relationship with my cousin. "But you are my family too. You are my sister."

"I'm sorry, Jay." Keisha hugged me. "Today is your birthday and here I am on some bullshit. Seeing Shawnie with that bitch...the shit hurts. You know he told me to stop contacting him? Talking about he trying to focus on his relationship with that basic bitch."

"I understand." I refused to get in the middle of Shawnie's weird love triangle. I was already in a weirder one with my sister and her baby daddy. "I want you to have a good time tonight... with Mr. Otis and your stepdaughter." I smiled.

"What the fuck ever. Do you think Shawnie is feeling some type of way about me and Bernard?"

"No." I shook my head from side to side. "Nobody is tripping about you and your sugar unc. But you are not here for that. You are here to have a good time with me. Bitch I'm getting married!" I held up my hand.

"That's what I'm talking about. I may be mad about Shawnie but I'm so happy for you, sis!" Keisha hugged me again.

"Get out your feelings and let's go fuck it up!" I pulled Keisha back into the main area as the DJ began to play "Best Friend" by Doja Cat.

Keisha and I got super rachet as we twerked on each other. I think the whole club seen my ass shake. I was fucking it up when Ice brought me into his space.

"Damn what's your name little mama." Ice rubbed his hands down my body.

"Jaya." I smiled as I took the blunt out of his hand and hit it. I was feeling like a fiending crack head because it had been forever since I smoked some gas.

"You got a man, Jaya?"

"No."

"Can I change that?" Ice asked as he took the blunt from me.

"What that mouth do?" Ice and I began to laugh.

"Don't get too fucked up. We got plans later."

"Is that right?" I wrapped my arms around Ice.

"I got a little something planned. That's all I'm saying."

"Alright." Shawnie and Dejah walked up on us. "We out."

"Congrats, y'all." Dejah smiled.

"Thank you! We probably going to leave too." I looked over at Ice. I was ready for my surprise. Ever since Israel was born six weeks ago, I rarely spent alone time with Ice. This was my first night baby free and I was ready to fuck a real one. We said bye to all our guests. Ice said they could stay in VIP until the club closed. Drinks was on him.

As soon as we stepped outside there was a Midnight Rolls Royce Cullinan with a chauffeur standing at the passenger door. As soon as we got into the back of the car the ceiling lit up with little stars. I couldn't stop smiling. I needed this so much.

The betrayal of my dad cut deep. Everything Trinity knew about me all the way down to my gender reveal, our dad told her. I had been depressed for weeks. Dealing with guilt of being with my sister's baby daddy, betrayal of my dad, and trying to stay out of Shawnie's fucked up love life, some days it was too much. But I could honestly say that my and Ice's relationship was getting better by the day. All this shit that was being thrown at us only made our love that much stronger. Plus, my daughter was the best blessing. She was a good baby and was sleeping through the night by now.

I tried to give Trap Star the chance to be in his daughter's life. But I ain't talked to him since I was six months pregnant. He's still fucking with Alisha. He swore I was trying to trap him with another nigga's baby. That's fine, believe that bullshit. I didn't want him to be my daughter's daddy in the first place.

I moved on with my life and I was happy. But I heard that Trap Star and my ex best friend, Alisha was out here doing bad. I guess krama is a bitch. I would have been less hurt if Trap Star would have come to me and say, "I'm not happy. I want to be with Alisha." I would have left. But for Alisha to play in my face about a fake boyfriend, telling me how fire the dick was, and how much she loved him, was below the belt. And for Trap Star to come at me like some hoe off the street, was fucked up. Instead of continuing to trip on them was waste of time. I got who I always wanted and even though Ice and I had been through hell to be together, he is my forever.

So when I had Israel I'Liana Green, Ice signed the birth certificate. There ain't a drop of Ice's blood that runs through Israel's veins but that's her daddy. These last few months has taught me that blood don't make you family and I was perfectly fine with the people I chose to deal with.

"Baby!" I screeched as the car came to a stop off the coast of the Miami South Channel. The bay was filled with large yachts.

"Come on." Ice grabbed me by the hand as the chauffer opened the door. All of my life I lived in Florida, and I've never been on a yacht. I was geeked as I tried to take in the beauty of the massive yachts.

"You want to get into the hot tub?" Ice asked as soon as we got on the yacht named Sunshine.

"I don't have a swimming suit." I pouted. I was wild but not wild enough to get naked in front of the yacht staff.

"Dejah packed you a bag. It's in our room." Ice led the way down the stairs to the state rooms.

I wanted to get in the jacuzzi, but I had to first thank my fiancé for this amazing night.

"If you're hungry..." Ice stopped talking as I dropped to my knees and began to unzip his pants. Ice bit down on his lip as he watched his dick disappear into my mouth. I was drunk, high, and horny. All my favorite things. It was the way my engagement ring sparkled as I wrapped my hand around Ice's dick for me. Some bitches didn't like sucking dick. But I did. Hence, why I got a nigga to wife me and claim my baby as his own. I was so good at it that it put Ice in a trance. I didn't have no tricks tonight other than my oral skills.

"Damn like that?" Ice watched in amazement as I spit on his dick. I didn't utter a word as we made eye contact as I slurped on Ice's dick like it was a bomb pop on a hot summer day. The way Ice grunted was making my pussy wet. Ice's hand found the back of my head and he snatched me by my hair, hard. My pussy was now leaking from his aggression. Ice leaned down and kissed me with his nasty ass before my mouth found his one-eyed snake again. Ice didn't let go of my hair as I continued to suck and gag on his shit. Ice's head swelled in my mouth, letting me know he was about to nut. I sucked harder as his cum coated my throat.

"You so fucking nasty." Ice lifted me up.

"And that's why you gave me this ring!" I cheesed and held my hand up.

"You damn right." Ice tried to snatch me up.

"Wait babe." I found the Bluetooth system and hooked up my phone. I put on my "Dick Time" play list. Keisha wasn't the only one that knew how to strip. I slowly took my clothes off to "Set Him Up".

For me to only have had two sexual partners, I was a straight freak. But good dick brought out the hoe in me and I was down with anything other than anal and threesomes. I was butt ass naked as I laid back on the bed and spread my legs open. My hand found my clit and my juicy opening. I let out a moan as my finger slipped in my wet, tight, pussy. The shit felt good as I plunged my finger in between my sugar walls. Now I was seeing why Ice was so addicted to this pussy. I had that WAP for real. I was so caught up in pleasuring myself that I forgot Ice was in the room as he got in between my legs.

Ice moved my hand from inside my pussy and continued to rub on my pearl. He replaced my finger with his tongue and a burst of nirvana shot down my spine. This right here was why I gave no fucks about Trinity being my man's baby mama. Ice continued to fuck me with his tongue as I rode the wave of orgasmic bliss. Ice gripped my legs back and all I could do was whine for him not to stop.

As I was catching my breath I realized that my six-week appointment was not for another week. I wasn't on birth control and as much as I loved my daughter, I wasn't looking to have another baby any time soon.

"You got any condoms?" I stopped Ice before he dove in the pussy.

"Why would I have condoms?" Ice looked at me strangely.

"You're right. However, I'm not on birth control." I looked in Ice's eyes and his stupid ass smiled.

"No." I read Ice's mind. "I think you have enough kids."

"Okay." Ice tried to lean me back.

"I'm not playing, Isaiah. You better pull out."

"I got you." Ice kissed me as he tried to lean me back on the bed.

"Don't nut in me." I warned as Ice slipped the head in. Once half his dick was inside me, I forgot about what I was saying. All I was trying to do was catch this nut.

"Please God don't let me get pregnant." I thought to myself.

But the way I was cummin' back-to-back I didn't know if Ice or I had the will power to stop him from nutting inside me. As soon as I got off this boat, I was going to Wawa or CVS for a Plan B pill.

Ice had put both me and him to sleep. My ass was wore out. The next thing I know is my phone is ringing. I didn't even look at the caller ID.

"Hello?" I asked groggily.

"Hey baby girl!"

My whole body itched when I realized who was on the phone. "What's up Jayson?" I got an attitude.

"Oh, we on first name bases now?" Jayson asked surprised as he took his burner phone off speaker.

"You ain't my father no more. You made that very clear." I sat up in the bed.

"Jaya, I didn't mean for you to get hurt. I really didn't. I got a lot of shit going on. My beef is with Ice. Not you."

"If you got beef with Ice than you got beef with me too. And what about the fact of Trinity? My whole life you been lying to me. Why keep something like that from us? Your sister, your nephew, and me."

"I done did some fucked up shit over the years, baby girl. Daddy got a lot of skeletons. I want to explain everything to you in person. I need you to come see me."

"Say what you have to say now."

"Jaya, I want to see you. It's been months. And what I need to say, it has to be done in person. Make the visit."

"Alright." I huffed.

"Oh and Jaya?"

"Yeah?"

"Tell Ice that I saw his visitor request. Tell him in due time we're going to meet, but I want to see you first. I love you." The phone hung up.

I was speechless. I just wanted to live my life. Last night was everything. I had a good birthday, got engaged, got some dick and now this shit. But I refused to let this shit get to me. My dad had kept a secret of me having a sister, and deep down I wish that Trinity and I could build a relationship. But she was moving weird like our dad. But I could understand where she was coming from. Ice was fine, had money, and the dick was fire? Shit, I might have crashed the gender reveal too. I don't know if me and my dad could recover, but I was going try to see about building some kind of relationship with sister. The shit was so weird I didn't even know where to start.

ONE WEEK LATER

"You look so beautiful! Just like your mama." My dad hugged me as I just stood there.

As soon as he let go, I sat down. "So, how's my grandbaby? Why didn't you bring her?"

"We ain't on good terms, Jayson." I remained calm mostly out of fear. Last time I popped off the nigga had me dangling in the air like a necklace.

"We still on that disrespectful shit I see."

"You made it very clear that I wasn't your daughter. Did you try to break up me and Ice because you want him with Trinity?" I crossed my arms.

"Come on Jaya. You knew he had a girl and yet you didn't care. What makes you better than Alisha?"

"If I'm wrong. I'm wrong. But that shouldn't have you meddling in my love life. Ice don't want her. She had Izzy to trap him, and it still didn't work." I stated matter of fact. "They were only together for one month and she that pressed? Alisha was sleeping with my husband, not some nigga I only smashed three times."

Yeah, I had no business fucking another woman's man. I admit that. I'll take that side chick L. But I didn't break up no happy home. Alisha was fucking my legal husband; I fucked a man that been dealing with a chick for a month. There was a huge distance.

"I'm meddling because family should come before a nigga."

"I find out the day of my gender reveal that I had a sister from that supposed nigga. When something that big should have come from you years ago. How do you think I feel? You been lying to me my whole life!" My voice raised.

"You better pipe that shit down!"

Nothing had changed and I was ready to go. Deep down I thought my dad was going to apologize and we were going try to get back to what we used to have. But did we really have a good relationship since he's been lying this whole time? My dad would say, *"You're my favorite daughter."* And my dumb ass would say that *"I'm your only daughter."* Not once did he ever correct me. Maybe me and my sister wouldn't be in love with the same man if my dad would have introduced us a long time ago. Now we looked rachet. Now my daughter was going to be raised up with her brother/cousin. Shit I was my daughter's own auntie.

"Yeah, you ain't going to keep talking crazy to me." I stood to leave.

"Jaya sit down please." My dad beckoned, changing his tone like the Gemini that he was. I rolled my eyes, but I sat back down. "I'm frustrated about the whole situation. I got two daughters in love with the same man. As far as Trinity, that was my fault. I should have told you about her a long time ago. I was with your mama and I was with Trinity's mama. She got pregnant with Trinity and her dad was my connect. We got married because he forced me. I didn't tell yo mama because that's who I wanted to be with. I didn't tell anybody. Kimberly kept Trinity away most of the time and I was in here. I just didn't see a reason to stir the pot. To be honest, Trinity just got in touch with me right before you moved back to Miami." My dad stood up and walked around the table and hugged me. "I'm not going to pretend that I'm happy about you and Ice, but if this is what you want I'm going to accept it. I got a lot going on and I snapped on you."

I know I was supposed to be forgiving and I wanted to be in good place with my dad. But something wasn't right. I knew he was holding something back, but I just didn't know what. For one, my dad never held back from me, he always kept it one hundred.

Plus, I was told all my life that my parents met two years before I was born. So, if Trinity is four years older than me, how was he with my mom and Trinity's mom. Jayson made it seem like his love for my mom is why he's been keeping Trinity a secret and that was some bullshit. He should have been real from the beginning. And now I was feeling like I couldn't trust him.

The last time I was here my dad had me scared and now I was more scared than ever. He was up to something; I just couldn't put my finger on it. I can handle a vicious dog trying to attack because you see a dog coming. But with a snake, you never know when they will strike. Maybe my dad still loved me, but I was nothing but collateral damage with whatever agenda he had. As of today, my relationship with my father was now nonexistent.

9

SHAWNIE

"What's up with it?" I slapped hands with Lil' Way as I walked in Shanice's house.

"Same ol' shit. Different day."

"You got a blunt wrap?" I asked as I sat down on the couch and pulled out some gas.

"Yeah, roll up." He threw me a blunt wrap as I broke down. "Nigga I'm jelly." Lil' Way plopped down on the loveseat across from me.

"About what?" I briefly looked up from my task.

"Having sister wives. You and Ice. Shit at this point I would take some cousin wives."

"I ain't smashing Keisha."

"Nigga you ain't got to lie to me."

"Who is you? I don't have to lie, Zo. If I was smashing Keisha, everybody would know including my bitch."

"Shanice..."

"I know you ain't about to relay what your bitch told you?"

Lil' Way didn't have a rebuttal as my phone began to ring. "What's up?"

"He took Israel!" Jaya sobbed.

"Who?"

"Tyler took my baby!" Jaya choked on her words.

"What you mean he took your baby?" I wasn't following.

"Trap Star snatched my daughter!"

"Where's Ice?"

"I don't know. He's not answering the phone. The police are here..."

"Where you at?"

"At home. I don't know how he found out where I lived. He took my baby, Shawnie and I don't even know where to look for her at."

"I'm on my way." I ended the phone call.

"You good?" Lil' Way asked.

"Nah, this bitch ass nigga done snatched my niece." I no longer cared about the blunt I was smoking as I headed to the door. Lil' Way was on heels as I got in my whip. One thing about my niggas was they going to ride, no questions asked.

I made it to Jaya and Ice's house in record time. The car wasn't even in park all the way as I got out the car. I did not do authorities at all, but there was so many cops and channels 4, 6, 7, and 10 was here too. I had to park at the end of the block because there were so many vehicles.

"Excuse me sir, this is private..."

"That's my sister and my niece! I cut off the rent a cop.

"You're the uncle of Israel?" A news reporter from channel 7 asked.

"Yeah." I was looking for Jaya in a flood of people. I barely got that word out as news personnel surrounded me.

"Do you think Israel is in danger?"

"Do you have a current picture of Israel?"

"Who is Tyler Richardson?"

"Who do you think took Israel?"

"Is Jaya a fit mother?"

That last comment sent me over the edge. "What the fuck you say?" I looked at the tabloid reporter who had slithered his way into my space. It was taking every ounce of me not to go

Incredible Hulk on this bitch. I had to keep reminding myself that finding Israel was the priority and me going to jail wasn't going to help my sister or my niece. "Jaya is a great mother, Zo! Yo," I looked at twelve who had the house taped off with yellow tape like it was a homicide scene. "I need to get to my sister."

The cop didn't speak but let me and Lil' Way in. I found Jaya in the house looking like she had lost her mind and her heart. Her clothes were disheveled, hair looking crazy, and her eyes was puffy and red. As soon as she seen me, she wrapped her arms around me.

"He took my baby, Shawnie." Jaya cried drenching my shirt with her tears.

"What happened?" I pulled Jaya out of our embrace. I wanted to cry too but I needed answers to find my niece and I wasn't waiting for twelve for shit.

"I was getting the baby out the car and Alisha walked up on me and mace me. The shit got into Israel's eyes too because she began to scream. I fucking lost it as I tried to beat the breaks off that bitch. I couldn't see shit and that's when Trap Star came and snatched the baby. I fought him, I fought her. But I was no match for the both of them. I couldn't even tell you what car they were in. All I heard was my baby screaming." Jaya broke down.

"We going to get her back. You hear me?"

"Do you think they going to hurt Israel?"

"I don't think they would." I didn't know for sure, but I wasn't going to add fuel to the fire.

"This nigga swore up and down he wasn't the father and out of nowhere he comes and takes her? Why? He fucked my friend, kicked me out, divorced me, and he still trying to hurt me. I didn't ask that nigga for shit! I should have never told him I was pregnant."

I brought my voice down to a whisper so twelve couldn't hear me declare how I was moving. "I'ma get Israel back. Tyler is a dead nigga." I quickly hugged Jaya and walked to the door.

"What are you doing?" I stopped in my tracks as I seen Jaya close on my heels.

"I'm coming too."

I taught Jaya to be a hitta, but she ain't killed nothing but a marsh rabbit. Her ass was in tears about that damn bunny too. Her ass wasn't prepared for the shit I was about to do.

"Stay here."

"No..."

"You see all these muthafuckas here. You can't leave. Let me handle this shit. I'ma bring my niece home."

"But..."

"Where's Ma Dukes?" I changed the subject.

"She's on her way too."

"Bet. Stay here." I grabbed Jaya by her shoulders.

"I can't just stand here and not do nothing."

"You are doing something. I'm coming back with Israel."

"Okay." Jaya sobbed. "Find her Shawnie."

Lil' Way and I walked through the crowd of people, police, and news station vans back to my car.

"What's the move?" Lil' Way asked.

"When Jaya first got with the nigga, he was staying with a cousin in the Gardens. If he ain't there we going to Jacksonville."

"That's a four hour drive my nigga."

"And?" I mugged Lil' Way.

"Whoa!" Lil' Way shot his hands up in the air in his defense. "I'm not the enemy. I was just saying."

I called Ice a total of ten times as I walked back to the car, but the phone kept ringing. I didn't like this shit. He was supposed to be my niece's daddy. I know he was in these streets trying to get to the bag. But nigga ain't no bag more important than family.

"Where is Ice?" Lil' Way questioned as I heard the automated system pick up again.

That was a good question.

10

ICE

"Babe..." Trinity trailed kisses down my bare chest.

"You..." Trinity silenced my words by her kisses.

"The fuck?" I pushed Trinity back as I sat up in the bed.

"That last round wore you out?" Trinity tried to kiss me for a second time, but I blocked it. "We smashed?" I looked at Trinity oddly.

"All night." Trinity smiled.

"What time is it?" I asked more to myself than Trinity as I noticed I was naked.

"I think it's around ten in the morning."

"I spent the night?" I panicked.

"Uh...yeah."

"I got to go." I stood up to find my clothes. "Where the fuck are my clothes?"

"So you leaving?" Trinity got an attitude.

"I wasn't supposed to be here." I continued to look for my clothes.

"You are the one that came over here all drunk. Touching on me and shit."

I tried to think of last night's events, but shit was foggy. All I remember is dropping off my son to my baby mama. "Where's Izzy?" I questioned.

"My mom picked him up last night. Are you okay?"

"Where's my clothes at?" I had so many questions but no answers.

"Downstairs. I don't know." Trinity rubbed her pudgy stomach. "The way you was hitting it last night. Baby number two might be on the way. Hopefully, this time it's a girl. Make our little family complete."

"Nah, man." A nigga wanted to break down and cry like a bitch. I wasn't trying to have no more kids with Trinity. I looked around the room and there wasn't a condom or condom wrapper in sight. I was already fucking up by smashing Trinity, but raw dicking was some shit that was beyond foul. "Put your fucking clothes on! We going to go get a Plan B."

"I'm not killing my baby." Trinity snatched away from me. "You should have thought of that shit before you got between my legs without a condom." How the fuck was me and my baby mama butt ass naked fighting about a Plan B pill and I had a whole fiancé at home. Shit was all bad.

"Bitch..." I heard my phone ringing from downstairs. I jogged down the stairs to my phone. Of course, God wanted to make an example out of me because the word wifey was clear as day on my phone screen. I watched my phone ring like it was contaminated with a disease. I didn't have a good lie and the truth was a no go. The phone stopped ringing, but it began again, and it was Jaya. I rather have phone sex with Satan than explain to my bitch why I didn't come home last night.

"You better tell her ass you ain't coming back! You got your biological son. Not the fake baby." Trinity shouted from the top of the stairs.

"Bitch, say something else and I'm forget you're a woman!" I took a deep breath and answered the phone. "Baby?" I cringed.

"Tell that..." I hurried up and snatched up Trinity since she was now in my space while simultaneously putting my phone on mute.

"Do it look like I'm fucking playing?" I gripped Trinity's neck. "Shut the fuck up!"

"I'm not going anywhere baby daddy." Trinity wasn't fazed by my aggression.

I don't even know how I went from Isaiah Green to Chris Brown in seconds. Because I found myself punching the shit out of Trinity. "Take your ass upstairs! Now!" I shouted.

"But..." Trinity whined but her weird ass didn't seem upset.

I clocked my hand back like Ike did Tina in the sound booth and Trinity flinched as she backed away.

"Jaya?" I called back since Jaya had hung up. "My bad, babe the reception in here all fucked up. Twelve hemmed me up last night. But I'm on my way home..."

"Trap Star snatched Israel." Jaya cried. Now I was feeling lower than low. I'm smashing my baby mama all night and my daughter got kidnapped.

"You at the house?" I panicked as I tried to slip on my drawers.

"No, I'm at my auntie's house."

"Here I come." I quickly ended the call. It took a matter of seconds for me to put on my clothes. My mind was racing a mile a minute on where my baby girl was at. I wasn't understanding how I smashed Trinity when her pussy was trash. I don't even remember drinking and why the fuck would I be driving with my son drunk? A nigga was stressed but not to the point to be stupid drunk. I couldn't afford for Trinity to tell anybody that I was over here fucking while my daughter was being kidnapped. I didn't even want to think about the possibility of Trinity getting pregnant again.

"Trinity, don't you tell nobody I was here. And go get that fucking Plan B."

"I am not your sneaky link." Trinity crossed her arms over her chest in defiance.

I didn't have time to go back and forth with her stupid ass as I located my keys.

I left and was doing 90 mph as I drove to Keyonna's house. As soon as I pulled up, I seen Jaya sitting on the porch. My baby looked bad. She had on the same clothes she had on yesterday, her hair was fuzzy, and her eyes was blood shot red. Seeing her like this had my guilt at an all-time high.

I didn't know what to say as I approached the porch. "I don't even want to ask you where you been. I'm just trying to get my daughter back." Jaya moved away from me.

"I was in fucking jail!" I lied. "We can fight about that shit later. What is twelve saying?" I needed to know what they were doing to find my baby.

"They are looking for Israel. Shawnie and Lil' Way went to Jacksonville to find my baby. They ain't found shit. He ain't at home. He ain't at his cousin's down here. I don't know where to start looking. All I been doing is driving around. The police want me to stay put. But how can I just sit here when my baby is out there? The police said I'm in the way, so Auntie Key made me come over here since the police are in and out our house. Auntie Key took my keys. But I don't give a fuck, give me your keys." Jaya put her hands out.

"Jaya Leray Mitchell. You ain't going no fucking where. Let the police do their job." Jaya's auntie came out the house.

"They ain't doing a good job. Because where is my baby? Y'all don't want to help, I will walk." Jaya jumped off the porch so fast.

"Don't just stand there! Stop her!" Keyonna yelled at me.

I tried to stop Jaya, but she swung on me. "Auntie Key called the jails and the hospitals last night. I'm looking for my daughter and I'm worried something happened to you. Funny thing is, there wasn't an Isaiah Green in custody in the whole state of Florida. Go do what you been doing, Ice." Jaya stormed off.

"I gave them a fake name." I pulled another lie out my ass. "They gave me a PR bond this morning. I ain't never went without answering my phone. But they had me in a cell. I didn't even see the Amber alert because I was in jail."

"Whatever." Jaya dismissed me. "If you ain't going to help me then move out my way."

"Let's go find our daughter." I ignored the guilt that had settled in my gut.

God please bring Israel home safely.

11

JAYA

EIGHT DAYS LATER

I was past the brink of insanity. It had been eight days and my daughter was still gone. I wasn't eating. The only reason why I was sleeping was because my body crashed after three days of no sleep. I've been all over Florida. I didn't have any more tears and all I thought about was my child's safety.

The "What if" plagued my mind. Instead of swinging on Alisha I should have been grabbing Israel. My face was on fire and I was blind, but I still tried to follow them in my car. I crashed into a fucking tree. I wasn't even thinking about calling anybody. But the neighbor saw that I parked into their tree and called twelve. I think I knocked myself out because the paramedics was asking me a bunch of questions about my wellbeing. I didn't care about my wellbeing and all I wanted was to find my daughter. I was feeling like a failure as a mom. I blamed myself for having a baby by a bitch ass nigga.

"Jaya eat, baby." Auntie Key tried to feed me some gumbo.

"I'm not hungry." I moved my face.

"Channel 10 is on scene with breaking news..."

"Jaya it's been two days since you ate something. You can't

look for Israel if you in the hospital for malnutrition." Auntie Key tried to reason.

"What was first believed to be debris has been identified as a female infant child..."

I let out a breath of frustration as I took a few bites. My auntie was right, if I was in the hospital how was I going to find my daughter.

"Eight days ago, two-month-old Israel Green was taken from her South Miami home when her non-custodial father maced her mother and took baby Israel. Channel 10 is waiting for police to confirm the body of Israel..."

Hearing Israel's name triggered me to pay attention to the TV. I watched in horror as the news cameras zeroed in on a paramedic loading a small body bag unto a gurney.

"No...no." I dropped to my knees as my tears fell.

Auntie Key wrapped her arms around me as she cried too.

Okay, God I was ready to wake up. I don't want to play no more. I don't know what the lesson was, but I learned whatever you wanted me to learn. I know you are not supposed to question God but I wasn't understanding why my child was gone. I played no games about my daughter and I wasn't seeing why I was being punished. I smoke more weed than Snoop Dogg, but I stopped when I found out I was pregnant. I see bitches all the time mistreat, neglect, and abuse their kids and nothing ever happened to them. I was blinded by mace, crashed into a tree, and was unconscious for at least ten minutes and yet none of that shit deterred me from looking for Israel.

Black girls are supposed to be the epitome of strength. But I was tired. I was tired of being mistreated. I was tired of going through bullshit. As soon as shit got good, something came and fucked it up. All I knew was that by end today I was going to be joining my daughter in the afterlife. I had nothing to live for anymore.

I was crying one second and the next my body began to shake. I guess I didn't have to wait to meet my baby girl. I could hear Auntie Key screaming for me to hang on but for what? I was meeting up with Israel. I didn't fight the weirdness that shot through my body as I embraced the darkness.

I'm coming baby girl. Mama is coming.

"Jaya?" I heard a sweet voice call my name.

I made it. I was in heaven. All I needed to do was find my daughter. I fought to open my eyes and was highly disappointed to see that I was in a hospital bed. The nurse patted my hand. I looked past her to see Shawnie, Dejah, Auntie Key, Tia, and Ice standing behind her. Pity and despair plagued their faces as they all looked at me.

"You got to slow down mama. You were severely dehydrated and had a seizure. How are you feeling? Are you in any pain?"

"N..no" My voice felt like I rubbed my throat down with sandpaper. "I have to find my daug..." I stopped myself as the images of the body bag penetrated my mind. Tears filled the rims of my eyes like a bucket in the rain. I didn't even want to admit to myself or anybody that my daughter was dead. I couldn't wait to get my hands on Alisha and Tyler because they was some dead bitches!

I just stared into space trying to blink away the tears. I didn't know what my next move was. I still wanted to die but I had to kill my ex-husband and his shone first. The pain didn't lessen because I felt empty, alone, and a failure because I couldn't protect my baby.

"They found a baby off highway 95. But it wasn't Israel." Ice approached me with caution. I let out a breath of relief.

"So where is my baby?" I asked with anticipation.

"We don't know." Ice dropped his head.

I don't know why but I began to laugh hysterically. Everybody just stared at me. Yeah, a bitch had finally snapped. But by this point I didn't give a fuck. It was like I went from hell to hell, then back to hell. My baby was kidnapped, then I thought she was dead, but now she is still kidnapped. I couldn't catch a break.

How was Tyler to know how Israel liked to be hummed to? That when she got fussy to run the vacuum? Or that she rather have her back rubbed instead of patting her when she needed to burp. Was Alisha pinching my baby? Was Israel crying for me?

"Jaya…" The nurse tried to speak to me.

"I'm fine." I reassured the nurse as I snapped back into sanity. "Can you give me a minute with my family?"

"Yes." The nurse smiled tightly.

As soon as the door closed. "There is no way this nigga just disappeared into thin air." I spoke as I looked around the room for my belongings. I seen my phone and reached for it. My family didn't know what to think as they just watched me.

I don't know why I haven't been made this phone call. I needed someone who's reach was beyond the police. I would team up with the devil if it meant finding my daughter. I scrolled through my phone for what I was looking for and double clicked the unsaved number.

"Daddy?" If I wanted my father's help, calling him by his first name wasn't going to cut it. The pain of not knowing my daughter's location had humbled me like a muthafucka.

"It's about time you called. I saw the news. Daddy got you. Give me twenty-four hours and I'ma deliver my grandbaby and that nigga's head."

My dad may have been a lot of things, but he was a man of his word. "Thank you." I genuinely spoke.

"You ain't got to thank me baby girl. We family. I love you. I don't care if you mad at me, I'ma still look out. I'm not the enemy. The nigga in your bed is. He wasn't in jail, Jaya."

"How do you know…"

"I ain't the king of Miami for nothing. Keyonna called me and wanted to see if I knew anything about Ice being in jail. But she didn't tell me Israel was missing. I know a few niggas at the precincts. And nobody fitting Ice's description was taken in custody let alone arrested that night. I'm not trying throw shade, but I ain't trusting nobody right about now when it comes to you and my grandbaby."

I was soaking up everything my dad was saying like a sponge as I stared at Ice. I was peeping shit and Ice wouldn't look me in the eye.

Was I really sleeping with the opps? And if so, where was Ice the night Israel was kidnapped?

ஒ௫௫

ONE DAY LATER

Instead of being out there looking for my daughter, I was stuck in the hospital. Apparently, severe dehydration causes health issues. I was mentally not okay and the way they had me hooked up to these machines I wasn't doing good physically either. All I knew was depression.

"Hi..." I was sitting there staring into space when I seen Trinity walk into the room.

I didn't speak as stared at Trinity.

"I know I'm not the person you want to see right now. And I know that things haven't been the best between us. I seen what has been going on, on the news. No matter what, Israel is my niece and you are my sister. I'm here for you." Trinity patted my leg.

I was numb with grief and sat there just blinking. "Daddy is going to find her, Jaya. I don't know how, but I believe he isn't going to rest until he does." Trinity wrapped her arms around me in a hug. "I thought I wanted Isaiah. But he loves you. Plus, I rather have my sister than some man."

Two weeks ago, I would have been all about connecting with my sister. But my focus was on Israel. I didn't have energy for nothing else. It had been eleven days and I was losing hope. These eleven days was feeling more like eleven years.

"The fuck?" Ice stepped in the hospital room and looked at Trinity. I was just a shell of myself as Trinity and Ice began to exchange words. "What the fuck are you doing here?"

"I'm checking on my sister!"

"You just being nosy." Ice turned his attention to me. "You need anything, bae?"

"Israel."

"I know." Ice kissed my forehead. "We going to find her."

"Jaya you want some water?" Trinity offered as she poured water into my cup from the water pitcher. I reached for the cup and it felt so good going down my throat.

"How's my favorite patient?" The nurse walked in.

"I want my daughter..." If I wasn't so heavily sedated, I would not be sitting in this bed. I was just a zombie stuck in hell. I was aware of everything going on, but I was in mental bondage. This Seroquel the doctor gave me was no joke. They gave me something for me to sleep and when I wasn't sleep, I just stared off into space.

I'm ready to leave this fucked up dream, but every morning was a new day in hell.

12

DEJAH

"Damn you thick!" The man rubbed his hand down my back as he whispered in my ear to drown out the loud noises of the club.

"What's up? I'm trying to see what's going on." I eye fucked his bitch.

"You feeling my bitch?" Ole boy asked.

"I'm feeling both of y'all. So what's up?"

"Say less." He grabbed my hand.

"My place or yours?" I questioned as I played in his Kodak Black inspired hairstyle aka wicks.

"Mine." Trap Star draped his arms around me and Alisha. It took everything in me not to push Trap Star's nasty ass off of me. I fucked with Jaya but her ex-husband was trash. It was one thing to get done dirty by a fine ass nigga, but to get played by this black ass gremlin, I was not understanding. Her ass was really crying about this loser. How was this nigga getting bitches? It had to be the dick and money because there was no way. Thankfully, Israel looked like Jaya.

And don't even get me started on Alisha's busted ass. Life was whooping this bitch's ass. Edges thinner than a white bitch's lips and I think I was detecting a hint of fresh caught catfish coming from between Alisha's legs. Her twerk wind had me gagging, the shit was so bad that she had everybody around her removing themselves from the area. You don't need to use a gun to clear out the party, all you need is Alisha to open her legs.

Jaya wasn't sleeping and neither was Shawnie and Ice. Babe was on Florida's hat behind his niece. Even Jaya's dad had niggas looking. But Ice and Shawnie was taking no breaks in finding Israel. So, when Trap Star posted a pic of him and Alisha on the gram at Club Envy in Fort Lauderdale, Shawnie woke me out of bed. I got halfway dressed in the car. I didn't have any make-up on but that dark melanin was popping with some lip gloss. Between Trap Star's ugly ass and Alisha's ass it was entirely too much. But I was willing to do this shit for the team if it meant getting Israel back.

"You got some gas money?" Trap Star asked as we got outside.

"And I'm hungry." Alisha spoke up.

"Now what kind of shit is this?" I thought to myself.

"Uh yeah." I stopped to go through my purse to kill time. I wish Shawnie and Ice would hurry up because I was not getting in their car. By the way Trap Star was asking me for money, this hooptie, and how busted Alisha was looking the nigga had fell off.

"Where's my daughter at?" Ice popped out with his Ruger pointed at Trap Star's head. Before Alisha could react, babe had snatched her up.

"What the fuck is that?" Shawnie scrunched up his nose. "Babe you grabbed some crab legs?"

"No, that's her." I pointed to Alisha.

"You divorced my sister over shrimpy? Yo, where the fuck is my niece?"

"What are you talking about?" Trap Star played stupid.

"Tie them up babe." Shawnie instructed me as I pulled out the zip ties out of my purse. I worked silent and fast to secure both Trap Star and Alisha's hands.

"Walk!" Ice demanded as he took the gun and shoved it in Trap Star's back. I hit the trunk button of my car as we approached the back of my 2015 Nissan Altima.

"Don't worry, I'ma replace the car." Shawnie reassured me as I placed the duct tape from my purse on Alisha's mouth. But when I got to Trap Star he gave me a weird grin before he spit in my face. I felt so gross and before I could react, Shawnie's fist was slamming into Trap Star's face.

"You got some wipes?" Shawnie soften as he shoved Trap Star in my trunk.

I had some make-up wipes and some hand sanitizer. I doused the wipe in hand sanitizer and whipped my face. I was hot as I took my anger out on Trap Star's face.

"Chill." Shawnie stopped me.

"Where the baby at?" Ice ripped off the duct tape form Alisha's mouth causing Alisha to welp out in pain. I guess she wasn't answering fast enough, and Ice shoved Alisha in the trunk with his hands around her neck. "Where's my daughter!" Ice lost control.

"Bro, the dead don't talk." Shawnie tried to calm Ice down.

"She's at the motel." Alisha choked out when Ice finally let her go.

"Which one?" Ice grabbed Alisha by the collar.

"The...the Link." Alisha words stumbled out. "Please don't hurt me. I..." Ice closed the trunk on Alisha in mid-sentence.

"Let's ride." Shawnie snatched my keys from my hand as I followed. "Here take my keys. Go to my house."

"I thought we was doing this together?" I pointed between Shawnie and me. I drunk a red bull, I was going use the heel of my stiletto to stab a muthafucka, I was on my killer shit. Keisha wasn't the only one that could keep up with Shawnie. I was a rida too.

"I know. But this ain't Fort Nite. This is real life. And you don't need to be a part of that. I'ma see you in a minute."

Shawnie left me standing there as he and Ice took off in my car with Lil' Way following close behind.

I hope that Israel was okay. I wanted to call Jaya so bad and tell her that they were closer to finding the baby but I didn't want to say anything if shit went bad. I took a deep breath and hoped in Shawnie's truck.

❧ 13 ❧

ICE

The Link Motel was a hole in the wall. If it wasn't for Jayson's bitch ass we wouldn't even know that Trap Star and Alisha was in Fort Lauderdale. He didn't have their exact location, but the streets talk and found out that Trap Star got some work through some nigga he knew. To be honest, the shit sounded far fetch. As big as Florida was, Jayson being in prison, and you just so happen to know the guy that sold drugs to Trap Star? Something wasn't right. But I had to deal with one battle at a time. And my only focus right now was finding my daughter and getting her back to her mama.

When Jaya first got with Trap Star, the nigga had money. But this nigga was out here looking bad. Eyes glossy, crust in the corner of his mouth, face sunken in, I know a crackhead when I see one. Trap Star and his bitch was tweaking. But all this was fucking karma. You can't do people wrong and expect shit to go well.

I ran up the three flights of stairs to room 348, the room Alisha said that they were staying at. Before I put the room key that I took from Alisha in the lock, I could hear my daughter screaming from the other side of the door. I frantically pulled out my gun and slowly open the door, pointing my gun into the dimly lit room. I looked in the dingy bathroom and closet before I picked up a crying Israel off the bed. The shit had me pissed off. These bitch ass muthafuckas left my daughter by herself while they turned up. As soon as I picked Israel up she stopped crying. It was like she took a deep breath of relief. No telling how long she was here alone.

I was more than hot and as much as I wanted to take my daughter back to her mama, I needed to handle Trap Star and Alisha first. I found Israel's pacifier and washed it off. I gave Israel the pacifier and put her in the car seat.

"Let's take them to the trap." I spoke as I walked up on Lil' Way and Shawnie.

Shawnie and Lil' Way nodded their heads before heading back to Miami.

Israel was sleep in the car seat as I tied up Trap Star to a chair down in the basement of the trap.

"Nigga what are you about to do? That's my daughter." Trap Star smirked. "You mad Jaya wants me. Huh? Bitch been blowing up my phone."

I didn't even acknowledge Trap Star's attempt to get under my skin. He was a crackhead about to die. Nigga couldn't say shit to me. Jaya was blowing up his phone to get her daughter back. The nigga was delusional. Hell, he was already dead when he decided to take Israel.

"I'ma get Israel to her mama." I slapped hands with Shawnie and Lil' Way.

"Bet. I'll hit you up when I'm done."

I was more of a calm type of killer, I liked guns and that was my only method of killing. But Shawnie liked to be creative, especially when it came to family. Shawnie been wanting to kill Trap Star and I doubt that he was going to be using a gun. Especially when the nigga brought out some knives.

"Way, hold out his hand." I heard Shawnie tell Lil' Way as Alisha and Trap Star begged for their lives.

They had finally discharged Jaya from the hospital earlier this morning. I got Jaya home and comfortable and I had been out in the streets all day and night looking for Israel. In these last twelve days I seen Jaya go from sanity to insane. Crying to laughing. Talking about Israel to not speaking for hours. This whole time she barely ate, she rarely slept. I hated seeing my girl like this. I wasn't sleeping either. I felt so bad that I was laid up with Trinity when my daughter got taken. I didn't even want to tell Jaya the truth. I was taking that shit to the grave.

"Babe?" I walked into our house because Jaya's happy aura made it a home. I found Jaya sitting in the dark on the couch. The shit looked creepy. I don't think Jaya had taken a shower or did her hair in the last twelve days. She was giving me black Annabelle vibes.

"Jay?" I walked over to Jaya and she didn't move. "Look." I held Israel.

It took a second for Jaya to realize what was going on. But as soon as she saw the two month old baby, Jaya snatched her out of my hands.

Jaya didn't even speak as the tears fell and she held onto Israel like she would disappear into thin air. Jaya held Israel out so she could look at her as I turned on the lights. Jaya kissed Israel all over her face.

I sat down next Jaya and admired the love Jaya had for our daughter. "Where's Tyler?"

"Shawnie is handling it." I responded as Jaya shook her head up and down knowing that Shawnie was on his ID channel killer shit. She knew how her cousin got down.

"And Alisha?"

"Same thing."

"I was going crazy. I was suicidal and homicidal." Jaya spoke as I brought her closer.

"Your dad told us that Trap Star was in Fort Lauderdale."

"How did he know that?"

"That's good question. We certainly need a sit down."

"I don't even know who to trust."

"What's that supposed to mean."

"I can only trust my cousin." Jaya stated matter of fact.

"You can't trust me?"

"No. Where was you at the night Trap Star took Israel?" Jaya turned her body towards me.

"In jail." I lied with a straight face.

"Okay run it back. You dropped off Izzy to Trinity then what?"

"I was on my way back home when I got pulled over. They found some weed on me and took me down to the station."

"How did they arrest you?"

"What? They slapped the handcuffs on me. Shit I don't know. That was almost two weeks ago."

My dad said that..."

"The nigga that told everybody I was your brother. The nigga that hid the fact that you had a sister all your life. That nigga?"

"Then how did he know that you didn't go to jail, then?"

"Do you hear yourself? That's what he does, cause confusion. I thought we was past paying attention to what Jayson says. He doesn't want us together. We got our daughter back. Trap Star and Alisha will never be a problem and you want to bring up some cryptic shit your dad said. I know you been through shit these past few days. I have too. But maybe you need some time to yourself. Maybe I'm not who you want be around." I stood up to leave.

"I'm sorry." Jaya pressed her forehead into my chest while holding our daughter. "You right. I shouldn't trust anything he says."

"Baby, I understand." I wrapped my arms around Jaya. "Shit has been tense. Go take you a warm bath, I'll order us some food, okay?" I took Israel out of Jaya's arms. "I love you." I kissed Jaya's forehead.

"Alright." Jaya stared up at me. "I love you too."

I didn't want to be a fuck boy. I didn't want to lie to Jaya about the situation. I didn't want to be added to the list of men that did her dirty. To be honest, I don't even remember what happened that night other than waking up naked in Trinity's bed. I was cheating and didn't even know I was cheating.

I heard buzzing coming from the coffee table and seen that Jaya got a text message. My fuckups had me nosy. I prayed that Jaya wasn't out here doing me like I had did her. I don't think I would be able to handle that shit.

Sissy Poo: "I'ma drop off Izzy at daycare and I will be there around 10am. Love you!"

I didn't want to see this bitch let alone have Trinity in my house. I was more nervous than a Klan member at a Juneteenth celebration. All I need was for this bitch to say we smashed, and shit was over for me and Jaya. I don't think she would ever forgive me. How the fuck was some trash ass pussy causing this much havoc in my life.

14

KEISHA

"Kesh, have you seen my pill organizer?" Bernard asked from the bedroom.

"What is that?"

"Stepmom you got fifty dollars?" Sydney wondered as she came into Bernard's kitchen.

"I can't be your stepmom if I'm only three years older than you, Sidney. Ask your dad."

I turned my back on Sidney to continue my task of making me something to eat.

"What are you cooking us, sweetie?" Bernard came in the kitchen kissing me on the cheek.

"I made me some shrimp and grits."

"You know I can't eat that because of my blood pressure."

"I didn't make it for you. I made it for me." I rolled my eyes.

Bernard was cool but more times than not the age difference was very clear. Especially when it came to sex. Every time we fucked, I had to wait thirty minutes for his blue pill to kick in. And how did he expect for my pussy to get wet from listening to Frankie Beverly and the Maze runners? Even before my grandma died she wasn't listening to that shit.

All he talked about was the greatness of the nineties and I was born in 1997. I was starting to think that I was having daddy issues, because it was starting to feel like I was dating and fucking my dad, and I had never met my dad. Bernard acted like he was both my dad and my man.

"What's up with the attitude?" Bernard looked at me calmly.

I was snapping for no damn reason other than I was unhappy. I was feeling like a bitter bitch because punk ass Dejah got my man and I'm over here with Mr. Otis. I hated when Jaya was right. I was acting out because of my emotions. I was missing Shawnie like crazy and me trying to make him jealous had backfired. He was getting married and wasn't thinking about me. I had to let him go. But at the same time, I couldn't get with niggas to make myself feel better. I had to be happy about me for me.

I didn't have no dad growing up. Just a bunch of "uncles" that spent the night in my mama's room. For as long as I could remember the only male role mode, I had was Shawnie. He was so mean when I was a kid, but he looked after me like he did Jaya.

I was this shy, timid girl that thought if I stayed quiet my mother wouldn't attack me. She wouldn't hit me because I was being a "good, quiet girl". Boy was I wrong. Not only did it not stop her from whooping my ass for things like there not being in the food in the house, it gave her last boyfriend the impression that I was easy prey.

Rodney was nice at first. But he seen that I was nothing but a broken girl living in a broken home. So, something like a meal and some clean clothes impressed me. And for three months, Rodney made sure I ate every day and got me a few outfits from Walmart. I thought he cared for me like a father because he didn't allow my mother, Charlotte, to hit on me.

All through middle school I fought almost every day because somebody was talking about me. They would say shit like I was dingy, poor, and trifling. One time I was in Spanish class and the teacher asked for this chick to name something red in Spanish, and this bitch said, "Keisha's nasty panties are roja." It didn't help the situation that I gotten my first period the week before and bled all over the chair. I got suspended for three days after whooping that bitch's ass. Nobody understood that my situation wasn't my fault. Like I wanted to be a dusty basic bitch.

And that's what Rodney seen; them Walmart clothes didn't stop the kids from talking about me but at least they weren't saying my clothes were dingy. But one night when my mom was passed out drunk, Rodney made his move. I thought fast and kicked him in his balls. I don't know how I got away, but I ran all the way to Jaya's house.

Jaya and I went to the same elementary school, but we didn't go to the same middle school. So I was on my own with the bullying. Even back then, Shawnie was a big nigga and he took me back home and shot that nigga dead in my house. To this day the police think it was a robbery gone bad or maybe they didn't give a fuck that another black man was dead. Either way, I was happy Rodney was gone. Shawnie had been selling drugs since he was thirteen and had always looked out for me, but after killing Rodney he really made sure I was good by making sure I had clothes, shoes, and he paid one of the crackheads to keep up with my hair.

So, when I say our love runs deep, I mean that shit. And not on no he saved me type shit either. I love Shawnie because he is my closet friend. I can be me and he saw my beauty before I realize I had any. I know he will never judge me and despite what he thinks, my loyalty is always to him.

I don't regret giving my virginity to Shawnie because he was and is still my everything. All of Miami knew that I was his and he was mine. Shawnie treated me like a queen. The money was good, but his love was better. I was willing to hold my nigga down while he was in prison and shit just went left. That whole

Tommy thing was me being hurt and not wanting to look stupid when I thought Shawnie was with other bitches.

But no matter how much I loved Shawnie, I had to move on. One thing I wasn't going to do is wait on the sideline like an old toy for Shawnie to realize again what I meant to him. He wanted dumb ass Dejah who allowed him to fuck everything moving. If I got to let my man play in front of me like that just so I can get a ring, I didn't want it.

"It has been a long morning." I matched Bernard's energy of calmness. Bernard had been nothing but sweet and here I was acting like a bitch. Even his daughter accepted me and I was being mean to her. "Give me a second to whip up you and Sidney some breakfast." I smiled.

⚜

I was back dancing at King of Diamonds but not tonight since I was going out with my bitch, Jaya. I was in a better mood since Bernard ate my pussy and gave me some money. I had my own money but I didn't turn down monetary gifts. Even having to wait for his blue pill to kick in didn't deter me from having a better mood. I don't even know why he took that damn thing knowing he couldn't last but thirty minutes in my WAP. Dick be hard for hours and he be wore out. I made sure to put his old ass to sleep with this pussy before I headed out.

He wasn't a bad guy. And I wasn't trying to play with his heart. Lord knows he was old. But I liked him and maybe I could grow into loving Bernard. It wasn't like I was entertaining any niggas. It was just me, Sugar Unc and my stepdaughter.

"Bitch you play entirely too much." I made eye contact with Dejah as I walked into Jaya's house. I was all about moving on but what I wasn't about to do was play like shit was cool between me and Dejah.

Jaya didn't even acknowledge me. "Thank you Dejah for

coming. I'll call you later." Jaya held the door for Dejah to leave and we mugged each other as she walked out. But I bet that hoe didn't say a word to me. Shawnie wasn't here to save her this time.

"So, since Shawnie replaced me you replacing me too?" I crossed my arms over my chest.

"Shawnie could never replace you and neither can I. She came over to check on me. I know you don't want to hear this, but she isn't a bad person. She's actually really nice."

"Oh, like how Alisha was? Was she nicer before or after she was fucking your husband?"

"I fuckin' hate you!" Jaya smirked as she rolled her eyes. "You right. A bitch could be Jesus' best friend but if you don't like her, you don't like her."

"Finally, you are understanding."

"Speaking about bitches you don't like. Trinity is going to meet us up there."

I had to look at Jaya crazy. "Trinity as your sister Trinity. Trinity as your man's baby mama, Trinity?"

"I know it sounds weird..."

"Because it is weird."

"But I've been getting to know her and we have so much in common. She really is the big sister I never had."

"Don't she want Ice still?" I was so confused as to why Jaya was kicking it with the bitch that wanted and had fucked her man.

"No. She's actually got a boyfriend now. We talked and she apologize for coming to my gender reveal acting stupid. She was hurt by Ice and doing dumb shit. But she wants me as a sister more than trying to get with Ice."

I wasn't falling for the bullshit. "This boyfriend, have you met him?"

"Yes! He actually is the brother of the little boy that Isis is dating from church."

"Bitch, Miami can't be this small. Shit, if that's the case is Bernard your uncle's neighbor's play cousin?"

"I don't even have an uncle!" Jaya laughed. "The boyfriend can be Ice's little sister's boyfriend's brother. As long as I'm no longer in a love triangle with my sister and her baby daddy."

"How does this shit even work? Like how is Izzy your nephew and your stepson? What does Ice think?"

"I never said it was normal. I don't know how we're going to work this shit out. Ice hates it. Every time Trinity comes over, he gets ghost. It's to the point that he don't want to interact with her at all and I end up going with him to get the baby."

"And you got the nerve to clown me about Bernard."

"How long do it take for him to get his dick hard again? An hour? No, it was two days and some jumper cables!" Jaya giggled.

"Fuck you!" I got a faux attitude. "When he do get it hard, just know he be having me nutting."

"But don't you have to hose him down to get it unhard?"

"See fuck this, I'm leaving." I walked towards the door, but Jaya tugged on me not being able to contain her laughter.

"I'm sorry." Jaya tried to stop giggling.

"I miss this smile." I admired my best friend's joy. When Israel was missing, I thought my friend was gone. But to see her back to normal was a blessing.

"I do too." Jaya smiled all goofy causing us to both giggle. "Let's hit these streets before Ice and Israel get home. We outside bitch!"

It felt good to be out with Jaya as we got lit at the bar in downtown Miami.

I was drunk and so was Jaya. We needed this best friend time.

"Trinity can't make it. She ain't feeling good." Jaya stumbled over here words as she looked down at her phone.

"Good. I don't trust that bitch anyway."

"You don't trust nobody! You remember that time I came..." Jaya started but fell face first onto our table. This bitch was drunk, drunk.

"Jay? Jaya?" I nudged Jaya but all I got was some soft snoring in return.

I was too drunk my damn self to drive us home and we drove Jaya's car here. "Can I get another 1942 and pineapple juice." I told the bartender, but she was staring at Jaya's passed out ass. "It's for me."

I was going to drink a little bit more until I figured out how to get me and Jaya home. Before I could finish my drink, Shawnie was calling Jaya's phone.

"Can you come get us?" I slurred my words as I answered her phone.

"Who is us?"

"Me and Jaya. We at Cameo off 14th and Washington Avenue."

"I'm on my way." Shawnie hung up on me.

Twenty minutes later Shawnie was calling my phone to tell me he was outside. I had maneuvered Jaya to walk since Shawnie had his gun on him and would not be admitted into the club. "Wake up bitch!" I tried to wake up Jaya, but her ass was no good. By the time I got outside both Shawnie and Ice was standing out front.

"If I knew her ass was this drunk. I would have come in and got her." Ice commented.

As soon as Jaya heard Ice's voice she woke up. "Baby!" Jaya slurred as she tried to kiss Ice but stumbled backwards.

Ice began to lead Jaya to her car, and I followed.

"I was here to take your funny looking ass home." Shawnie said from behind me.

"Whatever." I turned around to walk with Shawnie to his truck.

"Are you going home or you going to Papa Clarence's house?"

"His name is Bernard." I responded as we got in Shawnie's truck. "And I'm going home."

I don't know if It was the liquor buy Shawnie was looking extra sexy. He must have gotten his dreads re-twisted, he was in a white and black AMIRI shirt, Tom Ford jeans, a thick ass Cuban link chain, and Aurelian flat Christian Louboutin sneakers graced his feet. Not to mention the Aventus Creed cologne that had me soaking through my panties. A far cry from Bernard's starch creased Phat Farm jeans, Dragon shirt from Ross, and chucks.

"Quit staring at my dick if you don't want it shoved down your throat." Shawnie brought me out of my thoughts.

"I'm staring at it because I'm wondering how a grown big ass man got a baby dick." I clapped back.

"Yeah ok."

"You can just take me to Jaya's house. My car is there."

"No, we going to your house."

"We? Uh, I'm going home by myself, friend." I declared as we pulled up to my duplex.

When Shawnie killed the engine and hopped out the truck with me, I knew he was coming in, I just hoped he knew he wasn't cumming in me.

As soon as I got in the house I took off my heels and pulled my dress over my head.

"I thought you said you didn't want no dick?" Shawnie admired my body and I saw his dick swell in his pants.

"I don't." I stared at Shawnie's dick print as I bit down on my lip.

I quickly turned to go in my bedroom to stop myself from rushing Shawnie. Bernard dick game wasn't bad, but Shawnie was laying the pipe. "There's some blankets in the closet and a pillow." I spoke over my shoulder.

"Scoot over." Shawnie said to me as he came into my room only wearing his boxers. It was like God took some Madagascar chocolate and molded Shawnie into perfection. I was firm about not being the side chick but now my ass didn't know.

"Shawnie go home." I diverted my eyes.

"Why? You don't think you can resist me?" Shawnie smirked as he brushed his hand down my neck gripping it slightly. He knew that shit turned me on. His ass knew exactly what he was doing.

"Nigga, you smell like pickle juice and you musty. There ain't shit sexy about you." I rolled my eyes as I turned over.

"You know I see through all that tough girl shit. Just admit that you want me to pipe you down, Kesh."

I was hot in more ways than one. I was both horny and mad. Horny because I knew that Shawnie had that fire and mad because I was horny. "Bernard's name is written all over this pussy." I lied my ass off.

Shawnie began to laugh. "Yeah, ok. I'ma leave yo ass alone." Shawnie pulled me closer and draped his arm around me. "You been alright though?" Shawnie asked as I turned to face him.

"I don't know. Shit has been so weird."

"Who you telling? I feel like shit ain't what it's supposed to be. I love Dejah. But she ain't you. I'm just trying to do right."

"But are you happy?"

"I'm content. I'm kind of happy. If my ass was happy, I don't think I would be here with you."

Shit like this is why our connection ran so deep because we were able to talk like this. "I'm not happy either. I got with Bernard because you are marrying Dejah." I told my truth.

"Hell nah! I got serious with Dejah because you was still with Tommy."

"We got to stop doing shit out of pain. Maybe we aren't meant to be together because shit keeps coming up. I didn't think I would ever say this, but I want you to be happy. I want you to be happy with Dejah."

I felt a few tears fall. I was going to stop being selfish. I may have called Dejah a dumb bitch, but I had to finally admit that she loved Shawnie. Me nor Shawnie couldn't go back to change the past.

"But I don't know how to let you go."

"You have to." I let my lips brush up against Shawnie's before quickly pulling away. I wanted so bad for Shawnie to be in between my legs. But I didn't want to let my heart be intertwined with a man that was no longer mine. No matter how good I fucked Shawnie, in the morning he was going back to his girl. "Good night, Shawnie." I turned over and closed my eyes.

The next morning I woke to an empty bed. It was bittersweet because I finally put on my big girl drawers and stopped chasing after Shawnie. I was now living for me, Keisha Johnson.

15

TRINITY

My dad wrapped his arms around me and I was happy
to see him.

"So, what's going on?" My dad as we sat down.

I was so excited about my new news. "Jaya and I are getting
close. I can't believe that I used to not like her."

"That's good. I don't want y'all fighting. You didn't mention
about Bando, did you?"

"No. I don't want to hurt her like that."

"This shit ain't got nothing to do with feelings. And this
nigga don't give a fuck about nobody."

"I drugged Ice." I let my head fall. "He couldn't you know..." I
let my voice go low. "Get hard."

"The fuck is wrong with you Trinity?" My dad got angry. "I
told your ass to back off him. You worrying about Ice and we got
bigger problems. You slept with your sister's man?"

"No. He thinks we did though."

"You really not following the plan. I..."

"I know. I really don't want to hurt Jaya. I don't know how to
fix it."

I was so down to hurt Jaya at first. But I rather have a relationship with my sister than revenge. And to be honest, I was

actually happy. I had my son, I had my sister, and I had my new man, Kevin. Chasing after Ice had me bitter and depressed. I was chasing after a man that didn't want me. I let my dad put it in my head that I should be with Ice and not Jaya. Once I started to step back and concentrate on my son and me, things got better.

"Leave Ice alone. Did you give the money to Bando?"

"Yeah. What is the money for?"

"You asking too many questions. Did you find out anything about Trap Star?"

"Jaya said he kidnapped Israel. Wait that was the same night... Did Bando have anything to do with it?"

I was really hoping that the night that I tried to seduce Isaiah just so happened to be the night that Israel got kidnapped. I knew my dad kept his hands dirty but not to the point that his actions led to his granddaughter being kidnapped. I know that Bando was making my dad's life hard, but I've never seen my dad stressed. What did Bando have over his head. I wondered if he knew that Trap Star was smoking crack. From what Jaya told me, Trap Star left my niece in a motel room by herself. Anything could have happened to her.

"Daddy?" I looked at my dad as he held no emotion. He may have thought he was hiding his emotions but only a man that was hiding something hid their emotions. He didn't have to tell me; I knew by how he was acting that he was not in control of what was going on.

"Stick to the plan Trinity. You see how Israel came up missing. I would hate for that to happen to Izzy. I don't want to see my grandson's face on a t-shirt. These niggas don't give a fuck about you, me, or your sister. You know?"

I never met Bando, but I dropped off money to a house in Coral Gables. I thought my dad was just buying drugs. But I was seeing that was not the case. I couldn't keep with the plan of just doing what I was told of dropping the money off. I was doing too much behind Isaiah. I'm just glad that I valued the relationship with my sister more and my attraction to Isaiah no longer existed. I was with Kevin and I was happy.

I'm not saying that Kevin was a thief, but I let him spend the night and my weekly money drop off to Bando came up missing. I've been talking to Kevin for some months even before I had Izzy. But as shit got serious with me and Kevin, I let go of my feelings for Isaiah. When the money came up missing, Kevin swore he didn't take it and I believed him. For one he didn't suddenly buy an expensive car or break up with me.

I have yet to tell my dad and now I was wondering if Israel being kidnapped had anything to do with the missing money.

My mother was right, Jayson didn't care about anybody but himself. I was starting to have a change of heart about operation, *bitter bitch revenge*.

"You want to explain to me why Bando didn't get his money two days before my granddaughter's disappearance?" My dad brought me out of my thoughts.

"I lost it."

"What do you mean."

"Kevin spent the night. But he didn't take the money..."

My dad snatched my collar pulling me across the table like a rag doll. "Do it look like I'm fucking playing?" I shook my head no. I was crying and I was scared. "These niggas ain't playing! You bringing heat on the whole family because you don't follow directions! As of today, that little boyfriend is a dead nigga."

"Sorry..." I sobbed as my dad let me go. I was scared to move. I was embarrassed and I was hurt. I have become so close to my sister and I felt so bad that my actions had hurt her. Whatever bad blood we had before was gone. Even though I loved her, my dad had given me an ultimatum, either my sister or my man.

"Dead that bitch, ASAP!" My dad said callously.

"He didn't do it daddy, I swear."

"Don't worry about it. I'ma have that nigga dealt with my damn self."

"Hey, sis!" Jaya wrapped her arms around me as she opened the door.

"Hey." I said flatly.

"What's wrong?" Jaya asked with concern.

"Izzy kept me up all night." I lied.

"Where is Izzy?"

"He's at my mom's. You still want to go out to lunch." My voice began to shake.

"Yeah. You sure you're okay?" Jaya questioned.

"Yes!" I forced myself to smile.

My nerves were shot because I didn't want to be the reason why my niece got kidnapped. I didn't want to tell her but I had no choice.

My dad was a man of his word. It was like Kevin had disappeared. But I knew better and there was nothing I could do about it. I had to tell my sister the truth.

"Let me grab my purse." Jaya walked off as I checked to make sure the safety was on my gun.

Jaya and I decided to go to Sugar Cane.

"Can I tell you something?" Jaya looked at her menu.

"Sure." I swallowed hard.

"I want to thank you for being there for me when Israel was gone. You're a real one." Jaya grinned.

My heart was heavy. But I had to push through. "You're welcome. That's what sisters are for."

"I know this shit is weird but I don't care." Jaya opened her purse and pulled out a Tiffany box and a card with flowers on the front.

I opened the card, *"It's hard to believe,*
That in Just a little while,
I will be walking down the aisle,
And nothing would give me,
More joy and pride,

97

Than to have my favorite sister by my side.
Will you be my bridesmaid?"

"You want me to be your bridesmaid?" I had tears coming down my face.

"Do you mind that I marry your baby daddy?' Jaya joked and we both giggled.

"Yes I will be your bridesmaid!" I was so overwhelmed with being apart of my sister's special day.

"Open the box!"

I quickly opened the blue box to find a Tiffany charm bracelet. One of the charms had a "T" and another one said favorite sister. I couldn't stop crying. For one, because my sister and I was building a relationship. And for two, I was going confess everything.

"Listen." I looked Jaya in the eyes. "I have something to tell you. First, I want to say that us becoming close has been the best thing that has ever happened to me. And that's why I can't continue to..."

Pop Pop Pop

Was somebody popping firecrackers? I went to ask Jaya but I couldn't speak as she screamed over me as I laid on the ground.

"Someone call 911! My sister has been shot!"

"I'm not shot..." I spoke but no sound came out.

"Hold on Trinity!" Jaya cried. "Help is coming."

"Izzy." I was able to mumble out because it felt like my body was being pulled into darkness.

"No matter what I got my nephew."

That's all I needed to hear. I have done some dirty ass shit. I hurt a lot of people and now I was going to pay for it with my life. I guess it didn't matter that I tried to make shit right. What hurt the most was that I wasn't able to warn Jaya about Jayson. Little did she know that Jayson was coming for my baby sister. I failed as a big sister.

"Please God be with Jaya and protect over her, Ice, my niece and my son." I said a quick prayer as I was pulled into darkness.

❧ 16 ❧

JAYA

Some glad morning when this life is over
I'll fly away
When I die, Hallelujah, by and by
I'll fly away
Just a few more weary days and then
I'll fly away
To a land where joy shall never end

I sung my heart out as tears ran down my face like a leaky faucet. I still couldn't believe my sister was gone just when we were getting to know each other. When my mother died, I didn't even remember, but to go through this was too deep. But I made a promise, I would forever have Izzy.

I barely got through the song. As soon as I was done my dad was waiting for me with handcuffed arms. The prison let him out for furlough since his oldest child had died. I didn't care if two armed guards stood behind him and he was chained up. I needed my daddy as I cried in his arms. He was hurting too as he cried like a baby. It had become my dad's wish for his two daughters to get to know each other. I'm just happy that we were building something before Trinity died. My dad planted a quick kiss on my forehead and proceeded to stand up and do the eulogy.

"Trinity was my oldest child. I failed her because I wasn't there for her growing up. And now I failed in protecting her from this cold world. My daughter didn't deserve to die like this," My dad choked on his words.

"Take your time, Jayson!" Someone yelled out. I hated seeing my dad in pain. All the shit we been through in these last months no longer mattered. I forgave my dad and I wanted us to be close again to keep Trinity's memory alive.

"A parent shouldn't have to bury their child." My dad continued as the tears ran down his face. "My daughters are my everything. And now my only grandson ain't got a mama. Niggas are going to feel me about this one." My dad threatened. "Fly high, baby girl."

There wasn't a dry eye in the church when my dad sat back down. I was so glad so many people had come out. Especially my family. Both Auntie Key and Shawnie sat on the front row with me, daddy, Trinity's mom, and Kimberly. Ice refused to come. I know he didn't like Trinity, at one point I didn't either. But she was family and she was my sister, I couldn't keep a grudge for someone I didn't know.

After the services, since my dad wasn't allowed to travel too many places, the repass was done at the church. Plus, Kimberly didn't want all those people in the church at her house.

"You look just like your mother, Jaya." I turned to see Kimberly standing there with Izzy.

"Thank you." I didn't know what else to say. "Is that a good thing or a bad thing?" I wanted to know if she was about to throw some shade.

"It's a good thing. She was absolutely gorgeous."

My mind started to wonder. It was history repeating itself. I was the daughter of the side chick fucking my sister's man. Guilt had washed over me.

"She was a good woman, just got caught up with a bad man.

Just like me. You know when Trinity finally came to her senses, she wouldn't stop talking about you. My sister this, my sister that." Kimberly and I shared a smile. "She loved you. I'll tell you what I told her and hopefully you will listen unlike my daughter. You watch yourself with that one." Both Kimberly and I looked at my father as he talked with Auntie Key, Shawnie, and Dejah.

I didn't speak because me and my dad's relationship wasn't the best. But he was the one to find my daughter and now shit was complicated.

"Promise me you will stay in touch. Isaiah is Izzy's father and you are his fiancé. I respect that. And I don't want you or him to stop seeing Izzy. This little boy is going to need a village. I know Trinity would want the same thing."

"Thank you for understanding. And I promised my sister in her last breath that I would forever have my nephew." Me and Kimberly hugged it out.

"I'm going to go. I tolerated Jayson during the funeral but I can't be in the same room with him. Whenever you're ready for Izzy to come over, call me. Isaiah should have my number."

"What was she talking about?" My dad walked up on me with his entourage of armed officers.

"She wanted me to continue to be in Izzy's life. And that you can't be trusted" I kept my answer short.

"Oh. She's bitter that I chose your mama. She needs to worry about other shit. How are you feeling?"

"Numb."

"Yeah me too. We going to get through this together."

"Hey Unc, you want something to eat?" Shawnie asked as he, Dejah and Auntie Key came over to us.

"You already know that funeral chicken be hittin'." My dad commented.

"I know this ain't the time or the place, but you dead wrong for keeping Trinity a secret." My Auntie Key looked her brother in the face.

"Mama!" Shawnie tried to intervene but Auntie Key shot him

a look and he got quiet. Shawnie was a street nigga not scared of nobody but his mama. That's one person that could get him in check. High key my ass was scared of my Auntie Keyonna too. Shit, she raised me and I had the utmost respect for her.

"Keyonna don't start with me." My dad got defensive.

"Jayson don't start with me. I don't know what all you got going on but keep me and mine out of it."

"What are you talking about? You and Shawnie don't even come visit."

"It don't matter. And when I said me and mine. That included Jaya too. You are not going to continue to keep up bullshit from a prison cell. You know I don't hold my tongue for nobody. But as strange as Trinity was, she was family. And all that fighting her and Jaya was doing could have been eliminated if you would have said from the beginning you had another child. Do you got any more kids Jayson that we don't know about?"

All eyes were on my dad, even the two guards that was standing there were waiting on him to answer. "It's really not your business, but no. Trinity and Jaya are my only kids."

"It is my business." Auntie Key pointed at me. "Because I raised this one since she was four years old. And your two daughters were fucking the same man and didn't even know they was related. So yeah it's my business."

"You wilding." My dad commented back. I never seen him this calm. He hated for people to question him. I don't know if he was chill because he was in front of these guards or if he respected my Auntie that much. All I did was say I wanted to be with a man and he had choked me up. Even if he did help find my daughter, I still was feeling some type of way about how he had handled me in these last months.

My dad was checking all the boxes for me and him to be on better terms. And I'm a daddy's girl to the core. But something was off. I just couldn't put my finger off. The awkward feeling deep in my gut prevented me from bringing Israel to the funeral.

It stopped me from having my daughter with me today. I don't know why, but something inside just said it wasn't a good idea.

Since I got pregnant with Israel, all the men except Shawnie was showing me they couldn't be trusted. I may have seemed like everything was okay, but my guard stayed up. Ice was acting weird. My dad be acting weird. It was draining. I just didn't understand how you can love someone and not trust them. But that was how I was feeling about my fiancé and my dad.

SHAWNIE

"Baby right there." I moaned as Dejah straddled my back giving me a massage.

"You okay?"

"Yeah."

"With your cousin's death?"

"Jaya ain't dead." I was confused.

"No! Trinity."

"Oh. I didn't really know her. And to be honest, I didn't want to get to know her. Jaya was the only one on that weird Lifetime movie bullshit."

Was it fucked up that Trinity was in the wrong place at the wrong time? Yes. Some niggas were having a shootout across the street from the restaurant and the bullet hit Trinity. But I wasn't about be losing sleep behind a stranger. My family consisted of Dejah, my mom, Jaya, my niece, and my uncle. Anything else was irrelevant.

"I guess." Dejah commented. "Umm. I..."

"Say what you got to say." I was hoping that Dejah wasn't going to lecture me about me not giving a fuck about a stranger.

"I'm pregnant, Shawnie."

"Again? I thought you was on birth control?" I reached around to slide Dejah off my back.

"You think I'm trying to trap you?" Dejah looked at me crazy.

"Shit that's what it sounds like to me."

"Wow! You know damn well that ain't how I get down."

"How far along are you?" I stood up from the bed.

"I wanted to wait until I was out of the miscarriage stage to say something. But I'm three months."

"Ok...so who is the daddy? Cause I know it ain't mine."

Dejah scrunched up her face in confusion before it contoured into anger. "You are stupid!" Dejah through a pillow at my face. "My pussy been loyal."

"Miss me with that bullshit. Yeah this shit ain't about to work." I snatched open my drawer where Dejah kept her stuff at my house.

"You know what? Fuck you nigga! Bitch ass..." Dejah ranted as I threw a shirt at her.

I watched her eyes get big and then she started crying. "I hate you! You play too fucking much." Dejah looked down at the blue onesie.

I wrapped my arms around her in bear hug. "You act like a nigga didn't know them periods wasn't coming."

"So, you're not mad?" Dejah clarified.

I looked down at Dejah. "Why would I be mad for my baby having my baby?"

"You play too much." Dejah smacked her lips and rolled her eyes. "You had me thinking you was on some fuck boy shit."

I chuckled because I had Dejah thinking I was mad. It was taking everything in me not to laugh when I was going off. "I can't wait to meet my son." I kissed on Dejah.

"You ain't about to get no pussy, nigga." Dejah replied but she wasn't stopping me as I popped her titties out of her shirt.

"Put some clothes on." I got an epiphany.

"Where are we going?"

"To the courthouse."

"To do what?"

"We are getting married." I slapped Dejah's ass.

"What? JaShawn, I thought we was doing a wedding? You know, bridesmaids, a cake, a honeymoon? Our family being there." Dejah panicked.

"Get dressed." I shut that shit down as I laid Dejah on the bed.

"Dick isn't about to change my mind. You got me fucked up. I'm not doing that shit." Dejah declared.

❧

TWO HOURS LATER

"I ain't never met a chick like you. You done held me down through some fucked up shit. I don't even know how I lucked up with a woman like you. You my everything, Dejahnae. I love you." I spoke as I placed the ring onto Dejah's hand. Things were moving so fast that I had to cop some wedding bands from Jared's right quick before me and Dejah went to the courthouse. Even though things seemed rushed, this was what I wanted, Dejah was who I wanted. Keisha will always be a part of me because we been through so much together. But we both had to admit that we were each other's past. Dejah was my future, just like that old ass nigga was Keisha's.

"I was not prepared for this to be my wedding day. But I can't imagine being married to no one else. I love you so much, JaShawn. It has taken hell and high water for us to get here. I'm so blessed for you to be my baby daddy and my husband." Dejah was able to say through tears.

"Alright." The magistrate stated flatly. I guess he did a hundred marriages a day because the nigga wasn't hyped at all. "I now pronounce you Mr. and Mrs...." The magistrate looked down at our paperwork.

Dejah knew me to well and before I could knock this muthafucka out she was holding me back with her hand and pleading with her eyes for me not to go left.

"Is that a M or a N?" The magistrate tried to read my handwriting.

"Its Mitchell." Dejah tightly smiled; even though she was the calm one her ass was getting mad too.

"I now pronounce you Mr. and Mrs. Mitchell."

As far as I was concerned the nigga no longer existed as I wrapped my arms around Dejah's waist and brought her in for a kiss.

"How long do you think its going to take for you to plan a wedding?" I didn't forget about Dejah wanting a real wedding.

"Maybe a month." Dejah replied as we walked out the courthouse.

"Ok, whatever you want. I'ma pay for it."

"Ok." Dejah smiled. "So, what now?"

"You hungry?"

"Yeah."

"My mom cooked."

Dejah just looked at me.

"She is not going to be tripping."

"As soon as it gets weird, we leaving." Dejah declared.

My mom had cooked my favorite, fried chicken, baked mac and cheese, greens, cornbread, and banana pudding. I was planning on going over there today anyway. I was nervous about Ma Dukes reaction of not only me and Dejah getting married, but we were having a baby. I finally got Keyonna to tolerate Dejah. But she was still hoping me and Keisha would get back together. That shit was dead because now I was married.

"Why didn't you tell me you were bringing company?" My mom looked at Dejah as I walked into her door.

"Mama, chill." I tried to keep the piece. But Keyonna did what she wanted to do.

"Mama you didn't even look at your gift..." Keisha emerged from the bathroom.

My mom and Keisha were close but they have to calm down on all that. My mom was going to have to be team Dejah. Keisha didn't see me taking Clarence to his doctor appointments. We needed to sever all ties to each other.

"You about to go?" I questioned Keisha.

"No." Keisha sat down at the kitchen table.

"I didn't make enough for everybody. So..." My mom put her hands on her hips.

"Mama, you going have to stop acting like that. Dejah isn't going nowhere."

"You don't know that. I told your ass I'm not about to keep meeting a new girl every week."

"I ain't never brought home a bunch of shones." Ma Dukes was trying it.

"I'm ready to go, babe." Dejah looked at me. My mom was being damn disrespectful, but my wife kept it classy. I wasn't about to let nobody disrespect her.

"Alright. Let's go." I reached for Dejah's hand.

"I cooked all this food and you letting your little girlfriend make you leave?"

"She's not my girlfriend, we got married today."

"You a damn dummy." My mom commented. And what the fuck was I going to say back? Bitch, mind your business. "You and Keisha ain't fooling nobody. She with that old ass man and you got, *her*. Y'all doing this bullshit because neither of y'all want to admit that y'all stubborn. Now I ain't got nothing against Dejah. But she just ain't the one, son."

"She's the one because not only are we married but she is pregnant."

"If she the one, then why did you take your ass down to the courthouse and didn't tell nobody? Sounds like to me there's a dead cat on the line. Trying to prove a point you going to hurt everybody."

I wasn't about to hear this shit. No matter what I said, Ma Dukes would argue me down. I didn't even speak as I grabbed

Dejah by the hand and walked out the door. Dejah didn't say nothing but she was visibly upset.

"Nobody dictates who I want to be with. I don't regret getting married." I rubbed on Dejah's thigh as I backed out of the driveway.

"That's not what your mama thinks. She don't like me Shawnie."

"And I don't give a fuck! This my fucking life. Her or nobody else going to tell me what to do." I felt bad for Dejah because she was a good ass woman and she didn't deserve this shit.

"I guess you can just drop me off at home." Dejah didn't look my way as she looked out the window.

"Why would I drop you off to your mama's? We married so we live together. Let's go celebrate!" I tried to brighten the mood.

"I just want to go lay down. You know we can get an annulment if this is not what you want to do."

"Dejah stop talking like that. We came this far why would I switch up?"

"Because I'm not the girl you originally wanted." I glanced over at Dejah. "Maybe your mom is right. You didn't tell nobody."

"What you want me to do? Be like them lame ass niggas posting three paragraphs about they bitch on Facebook. Maybe my timing of all this wasn't what you expected but it don't take away that I wanted to marry you. Muthafuckas going have a lot to say. But the shit don't matter."

I thought I had made my choice but my mom was starting shit. No matter how I felt, I wasn't leaving Dejah and everybody needed to know that. Hopefully, my mom would stop tripping and give Dejah at least some respect. This was who I chose and muthafuckas better start respecting that.

✿ 18 ✿

ICE

"You don't think none of this is ghetto?" I whispered to my mom.

"Do you rather them be snorting coke and tricking?" My mom looked at me. "Be happy for your sisters."

My mom had convinced me to come see my little sisters' performance for church. I was all about someone getting to know the Lord. But my sisters was a hot mess as they did Tic Tok dances on stage to Kirk Franklin's Melodies from Heaven. I was so embarrassed to be their big brother. No fuck that, I blamed our mom. She wasn't the type to take us to wholesome family orientated events growing up. My OG was as hood as they came.

My phone began to vibrate so I walked out the sanctuary to take the call.

"Hey baby." Jaya spoke as soon as I answered the call.

I smiled. "Hey bae. I'ma be home as soon as my sisters' church performance is over."

"Okay. I sent you some pics." Jaya's voice dipped in lust as I got the notification that I got several pictures.

I looked around like everybody was going to see the photos. "Yeah you a freak.." I opened the pictures. I didn't see not one picture of Jaya but rather me butt ass naked laid up with Trinity. How the fuck was this bitch sending photos from the grave. Each picture was worse than the one before. Kissing, touching, there was even a video of Trinity sucking my dick. Most of the pics didn't have my face in them but it was me. Especially since the tattoos of my mother's name, my sisters, and the word "Ice" were clear as day.

"Nigga, didn't I tell you not to play with me?" Jaya's voice changed from sweet to mean as fuck.

"Baby let me explain..."

"This was the last straw nigga! You was fucking this bitch while my daughter was getting kidnapped? I'm up all night looking for my baby and you ducked off in some pussy. I should of killed that bitch my damn self the way she played in my face! But she got what was coming to her. But you nigga, I'm just getting started."

"Jaya. On my mama, I ain't cheating."

"Fuck you bitch!" Jaya hung up on me. As soon as the call ended, I heard glass being shattered outside. I ran outside to find Jaya with a crowbar breaking out the windows to my truck. She had already carved in the words, "Cheater" "Bitch" and "STD Nigga" into my vehicle like a pumpkin.

"What the fuck!" I was hot because my shit looked like it had been ran over with a semitruck.

"Do I look like I'm playing!" Jaya screamed as she made sure to put distance between us by standing on the other side of the car.

"Where's my daughter?" I tried to get Jaya to calm down.

"Nigga what daughter?" Jaya broke out the back window of my truck. "You ain't got no daughter no more!"

It was like the whole church poured out the doors to see me and my bitch's domestic issues. It was like Jaya got more animated for the crowd. By this time, I was chasing her ass around the car like we was playing musical chairs. "You fucked my sister nigga!"

"Her sister?" I heard one of the sisters of the church speak as everyone look at me with disgust.

"Jay this ain't the place to be wilding. Church? You really fuckin' up my car in front of Jesus?"

"You wasn't worried about Jesus when you was fuckin' my sister and my daughter was getting snatched."

"Jaya come on now." My mom came out the church trying to defuse the situation. "Isaiah loves you. Y'all can work this out...?

"Did Isaiah tell you he was fuckin' Trinity while Israel was getting kidnaped? He was gone all night and lied and said he was in jail. So, is this the reason you been acting weird?" Jaya looked at me.

"Son is this true?" My OG looked at me.

"Ma, I don't even remember what happened that night. But I didn't fuck her damn sister!"

"Yeah you did!" Jaya held up her phone so the whole church could see me sinning, ass naked with Trinity. "I don't have to lie."

"He going to hell." I heard another person say.

I was heated because I was looking like a bitch ass fuck boy. "Mind your business. Nigga what you going to do? Fuck all y'all!" I went off on the congregation.

But my rant was cut short as I seen from the corner of my eye Jaya throwing a lighter into the driver's side broken window. The flames ignited so fast and in a matter of seconds my truck was engulfed in flames. I lost it after that. I'd been calm but now I was seeing red as I charged after Jaya. I forgot she had that crowbar and she tried to take my head off with that muthafucka. But I was so angry that I didn't feel not one hit.

"Bitch who the fuck you think you is?" I grabbed Jaya by the neck. My aggression caused Jaya to pause but not for long before she began to swing on me again with that crowbar. I forgot her ass was a woman as I went to swing back but I was being pulled back by the men from the church.

"What the fuck is wrong with y'all?" My mom was yelling at me and Jaya.

But nobody was listening.

"Don't step foot on my porch! Everything you own is gone! Go stay with that bitch at the graveyard." Jaya yelled.

"Bitch that's my house!"

Jaya picked up my side mirror from the ground and tried to hit me but my mom grabbed her arms. "Come on Jaya..."

"Why you taking his side? He was laid up with my dead sister while my daughter was getting kidnapped." Jaya screamed.

"I'm not taking his side." My mom wrapped her arms around Jaya and she began to cry. I was feeling like shit.

"Who is the owner of the car?" Twelve came out nowhere as the fire department sprayed down my burning truck with water.

"I am, officer." I spoke up.

"Can you tell me what happened?"

"I accidently set it on fire." I replied with a straight face.

"You broke out the windows, wrote 'cheater' on the hood, and whooped your own ass?"

"Yes, officer." I wanted to fuck Jaya up but I be damned if I let her ass sit in a jail cell.

"That's the story you are going with?"

"Its not a story. It's the truth."

"Whatever." The officer no longer cared about getting to the truth. "You have the right to remain silent. Anything you say can and will be used against you.." Twelve turned me around to place me in handcuffs.

"Nah fuck that!" My mom shouted. "He didn't..."

"Ma, I got this. Just bail me out."

"I'm calling Chris now." My mom spoke about our lawyer.

❦

I only did five hours and soon as I got out I got an Uber home. I didn't even call my mom and tell her I was out. The night Israel got kidnapped was so hazy and I know that I would not have just fucked Trinity. Where the hell did them photos come from and who sent them to Jaya. I'ma go with Jayson's bitch ass for three hundred, Alex. Because I didn't have no enemies but his ass.

"Jaya?" I yelled as soon as I walked into our South Miami house. I searched the whole house and everything was there until I got to the bedrooms. All of Israel and Jaya's clothes was gone. Even her house keys and engagement ring sat on the dresser.

"Bae. What are we doing?" I asked as soon as Jaya answered the phone.

"I'm not fucking with you. Israel ain't your real daughter, so move on with your life."

"But I'm on her birth certificate."

"And?"

"Where you at? I'ma come get you."

"Nah, I'm good."

"I know it was your dad that sent you them pictures. We already know he be lying."

"No, they was in Trinity's phone. I was there when she got shot, remember? I got sad this morning that my sister was gone and wanted to see the pictures we took the day she died. And I found out how both of y'all was doing me behind my back. The pictures are very real. I kept asking you what happened, and you stood on that lie. Don't call my phone no more." Jaya hung up.

I tried to call back but her ass had blocked me.

"Fuck!" I threw my phone across the room in anger.

I'm glad I didn't break it because I forgot that I could track Jaya's phone. I seen her ass was at Keisha's house. I'm glad I had two cars as hopped in my whip and headed North. I was in luck because Jaya was walking to her car with Israel in her arms. She didn't even see me as I came from the side and snatched my daughter.

"Give me my baby, Isaiah!" I knew that if Israel was in my arms Jaya wouldn't steal on me.

"Get your shit because you coming home."

"I'm not going nowhere with you!" Jaya tried to grab the baby but I stepped back. "It's over. You foul. Give me my baby."

"You really going to let niggas come between us?"

"No, you did that. You the one that can't keep your dick in your pants. And its not even the cheating. It's the disrespect. I'm thinking something happened to you and you getting your dick sucked. I'm stressing over finding my baby and you out doing you. Well Isaiah continue to do you."

"I don't even know what happened that night. I don't remember. I wake up the next day not remembering anything. Her ass probably drugged me. I wasn't even attracted to Trinity. You know that. She said I was drunk but I left the house sober. I..."

"To be honest, I'm tired of hearing this shit. Its always something you did. You explaining why you doing shit you ain't doing. Every time I look up your name is coming up."

"And every time the shit came out it was your dad."

"Whatever and this time he wasn't. This shit stupid and I don't want to do it no more." Jaya reached for Israel.

"This is what your dad wants to happen."

"But you ain't making shit better. Give me my baby, Ice."

I felt defeated because Jaya wasn't letting up and I had no proof that I wasn't cheating. "So, what about the baby?" I still wanted to see my daughter.

"Nothing. You ain't the daddy." Jaya took the baby out my arms. The shit she just hit me with had a nigga feeling fucked up.

"She got my last name. I'm the only daddy she knows."

"She's still a baby she ain't going to remember. It's just best for all of us. You want Trinity? The dead bitch? You could have been said that's what you wanted. Have a blessed life." I watch Jaya walk back into Keisha's house.

Fuck, I really lost my bitch and I don't even remember doing shit.

✤ 19 ✤

JAYA

"I was ready to come out there and shoot his ass." Keisha stood by the window letting me know her ass was watching me.

"Its okay, I told him to just leave me alone."

"Well, you and the baby can stay here forever. My rent is only eight dollars."

"Thank you. I feel fucking stupid. And to think that my sister loved me. I even sung at this bitch's funeral and she fucking my man behind my back. I got the right mind to go to the cemetery, dig her up, and kick her ass."

"I told you I didn't like her. These hoes are grimy. I can't believe Ice is on that bullshit."

"Who you telling? Maybe my pussy be attracting cheating ass niggas." I laid a blanket down on the couch and put Israel on her stomach and began to pat her back so she can go to sleep.

"If that's the case, that's every bitch that walked the earth. It's the men. They don't appreciate a good woman. You know the best thing to do to get over a nigga? Get under a new one."

"Bitch I ain't you. And that type mindset is why you stuck with Mr. Otis." Keisha rolled her eyes. "I keep saying that I need to focus on me and end up doing the same shit. Not this time. I'ma stay at the food truck but I'll be looking for my own place."

"You know I know a guy that does real estate. He can hook you up."

"I ain't fucking no nigga for a place to stay."

"Bitch you was already doing that. But that's not what he is on. I promise. He just like to help out people. He helped me get this place on section 8. You know damn well I don't qualify for no damn three-bedroom duplex. But Ace hooked me up."

"Okay. Text me his number."

"I need to take a nap before I go to work tonight. You good? I texted you Dru's number."

"Yeah. Okay." I called the number as soon as Keisha sent it. I needed to stop depending on muthafuckas. "Hi, can I speak with Dru?"

"This is Dru."

"Um, Keisha gave me your number she said you do real estate. I want to see about renting a place."

"How much you have down for the deposit."

I swallowed. "Five hundred."

"I can work with that. How many people?"

"Just me and my daughter. So just two."

"What are you doing now? Can you come look at a place now?"

"Wow that was fast."

"I don't play around."

"Shoot me the addy. Me and my daughter are on the way."

"Alright."

Keisha! I'm going to meet that man about a place."

"Right now?" Keisha shouted from her bedroom.

"Yeah."

"I'm telling you now, the nigga fine."

"Girl I just broke up with my man a few hours ago. The last thing I'm thinking about is a nigga."

"You also said that when you came back to Miami. Got here and ten minutes later you was playing house with Ice."

"I've changed. I'll be back."

Keisha was a fucking liar because Ace was not fine, the nigga was fucking gorgeous. The nigga was so fine with his dark skin, deep waves, and almond shaped brown eyes.

"Jaya right?" Ace reached out his hand as I held one hand on Israel's stroller and the other to shake Ace's hand.

"Yes." I tried not to smile so hard.

"And who is this beautiful little girl?"

"This is my daughter, Israel."

"That's what's up. Let me show you the unit." Ace unlocked the door of the small house.

"I really appreciate your help, Ace."

"I'm all about helping people out. You can just call me Bando."

⊗⧉⊗

TWO WEEKS LATER

"I want to call him." I whined as I laid in the bed.

"Don't do it." Dejah warned.

"I need some dick!" I shouted. "I miss my man. I miss Ice."

Ace did what he said he was going to do and within a week I was moving into my own shit. I was so determined to be on my independent shit that I even bought my own furniture with my money. All I had was a couch, a coffee table, a bed, a crib, and folding table with some foldable chairs. But it was mine.

"Stay strong sis. Dick complicates shit."

"That's easy for you to say. You're getting dick every day."

"Not every day. I still got to deal with your crazy cousin outside the bedroom. Can I ask you something?" Dejah sat up in her bed.

I was at her and Shawnie's house, supposedly helping her

pack since Shawnie and she was moving next month. Dejah shouldn't have fed me first because now me and my baby was in her bed. Shit, Israel was already knocked out behind some mashed potatoes and a bottle.

"What's up?"

"Do you think that I made a mistake marrying Shawnie?"

"He cheating? What he do?" I didn't usually get involved with what Shawnie had going on. But my ass had nothing going on. Just two weeks ago I found out my ex-fiancé was fucking my dead sister. Today the only drama I had going on was that a snake was in my neighbor's yard. Life was boring as fuck right about now; I was intrigued to see what Shawnie and Dejah had going on.

"No! It more the fact of your auntie. She always saying slick shit. She don't like me and she makes it known that Shawnie should be with Keisha."

I already know how my auntie got down. She been loving Keisha forever. She knew Keisha's situation with her mama and she came to live with us after her grandma died. Even back then she was calling Keisha her daughter in law. Regardless of what Keisha and Shawnie had going on, it didn't stop my aunt and Keisha's relationship. I get it because I loved Keisha too. That was my bitch. She was a genuine, good ass person. If she was your friend, she was your friend. She ain't never been no sneaky, fucking somebody nigga on the low, backstabbing, shady female. She had a good heart.

I ain't gon lie, I wish shit had worked out for her and Shawnie. They belong together like the moon and the stars. You can't have one without the other. Keisha just brought a different type of man out of Shawnie. Nobody wanted to admit it except my Auntie Key but Shawnie was a happier man when he was with Keisha.

People didn't realize how close me and Shawnie was. Sometimes if felt like we were the same person or twins, we were so close. We talked. He stayed with Dejah out of loyalty. She was loyal to him, so he was loyal back. I'm not saying that he didn't grow to love Dejah, but his heart belonged to Keisha. And the only reason he married Dejah was because she got pregnant. He didn't want his baby to grow up like us; not having an active father in the home. Right now, Shawnie was living to make Dejah happy because he didn't want her to feel bad about how he really felt about Keisha. I guess I was the only one seeing the shit but every time it looked like he was going to go back with Keisha he would surprise Dejah with an engagement ring, flowers etc.

But I liked Dejah. She was good people. She loved Shawnie and she didn't pop off like Keisha. At first I wasn't fucking with Dejah because of my loyalty to Keisha, but now I fucked with both of them. But to be honest I was on whatever Shawnie was on. If he wanted to be with Dejah, I was going to rock with it. Keisha will forever be my best friend, but I fucked with Dejah.

"Can I be real with you?" I looked at Dejah and she shook her head up and down. "I think Shawnie does love you. I don't think it was a mistake getting married because Shawnie ain't the type of nigga to cheat or divorce. If he with you he with you. The shit is intimidating because Keisha and Shawnie been knowing each other since they were six and eight years old. There is shit that Shawnie would do for Keisha that he wouldn't do for anybody else. My auntie knows that. She been in Keisha's life for a long time too. She old." I tried to downplay the situation. "She's set in her ways. But she does like you...Just not as much as Keisha." I cringed as I told the truth.

"So basically, she ain't going to let up?"

"Hopefully by the time the baby gets here. But don't let that shit stop you from being happy. Do you think Shawnie is cheating?"

"No."

"See? Y'all good. Look at me. My ex-husband did me dirty. My ex-fiancé did me dirty. Girl, you winning. You got a good man that loves you and it be me and my daughter cuddling at night."

"Damn I'm sorry."

"I'ma be good. Shit I am. I miss Ice but I'm living my life."

"You miss me? So why you won't come home?" Ice stood in the doorway of the bedroom.

I rolled my eyes because I didn't want him knowing that I missed him. He wasn't going to keep playing me. "Nah, I'm good."

"You proved your point. You can do shit by yourself. Now come home."

"Go dig that bitch up and go play house with her."

"Y'all can't be having that light skin on light skin drama around my babies." Shawnie spoke about his unborn and niece.

I didn't speak as I mugged Shawnie.

What are you doing?" I looked at Ice like he lost his mind as he picked up Israel from the bed.

"I can't pick up my daughter, now?"

I smacked my lips. "Whatever."

As soon as Israel opened her eyes and seen Ice her ass started smiling. She was fake as fuck. "You miss daddy?" Ice cooed to Israel and she started that baby talk and smiling harder.

I was only in my new place three days before I relented and let Ice see the baby. I was hurt but he was right, he was Israel's daddy. He been in her life since I was three months pregnant, she had his last name, and his name was on her birth certificate.

"Jaya let me holla at you." Shawnie walked back to the living room.

"Yeah?" I crossed my arms over my chest.

"Ice wanted me to holla at you..."

"Not you too!" My auntie was already in my ear about working shit out with Ice.

"Ice ain't cheating."

"You saw the pics?"

"No. And I don't want to see them. But I was chopping it up with the nigga and he was saying that he was drugged. And I think he telling the truth. Ice know how to hold his liquor. My nigga ain't going to speak on what he be dealing with in these streets. But some nigga been moving in on a lot of his traps. And the ones he can't flip or rob, he been burning them down and Uncle Jayson been having to step in to help. Ice don't want you to know, so don't say nothing..."

"How is my dad doing that from a prison cell?"

"Why do you think we didn't struggle as kids? Mama working at Jackson Memorial as a janitor with two kids and we never went without? That was because of your dad. He help put me on. You don't think the whole situation is weird? Your daughter gets kidnapped and Ice gets caught up with Trinity in the same night. Me, Ice, and Lil' Way was in these streets day and night. But somehow your dad knows Trap Star is in Fort Lauderdale? Niggas tell the truth when they about to die. Trap Star said he was paid to take Israel."

"By who? And why you just now telling me?" I got mad.

"He didn't say. He was more scared of who ever it was than dying. But Uncle Jayson knows. I think he in debt to whoever it is. I didn't say shit because I was trying to figure out what is going on my damn self. I even tried to go see Uncle Jayson and the prison denied my visit. There is a lot of shit going on, but Ice isn't the enemy."

"When did you become team Ice?"

"Because I know the nigga love you. I'm starting to wonder if he only fuck with me so he can see you." Shawnie joked. "Y'all go talk or whatever. I got my niece."

"I'm good. I don't want to get played. Plus, why would Trinity do me like that."

"I don't even know. But Uncle Jayson probably got something to do with it too. He been moving real weird lately. Just hear Ice out. I don't think he fucked that girl willingly."

"So, if Dejah fucked a nigga unwillingly then what?"

"That means that's rape and I'ma kill that nigga. The bitch probably drugged him and raped him. But I know for a fact my nigga only want you. Since you been gone, he been drunk on my couch almost every night. Or he in the streets handling business. If he was on that fuck boy shit he would be knocking down shones. But he ain't Zo. Go home, Jay. You already know I wouldn't say that shit if I felt Ice was on some bullshit." Shawnie dropped his voice to a whisper. "I wish I would have listened to you and Ma Dukes about working shit out with Keisha. Now look at me, married and a baby on the way with someone who ain't bae. I don't want you to be like me. Don't give up on your forever, especially if they are not doing nothing wrong. I don't care what nigga is out there. Nobody going to love you like, Ice."

❦ 20 ❦

ICE

"Hi man!" I smiled at my son as he sat on the floor of Kimberly's playroom. I thought that she was going to be a bitch or weird like her daughter, but she was actually cool. She didn't give me a hard time about seeing my son. She knew what I did in these streets and she didn't judge me.

"How's Jaya and Israel?" Kimberly asked as she watched me interact with Izzy. "I've noticed she doesn't come with you to pick up and drop off Izzy. She doesn't take my calls anymore."

"Me and Jaya broke up." I commented.

"Because of Trinity?" Kimberly wondered.

I didn't feel comfortable sharing my business, so I kept my answer short. "Something like that."

"Trinity would do anything for her dad. But she learned later that she didn't want to do that. You know the night that Trinity died, I went to her house and I found out some things about my daughter. Things I was willing to go to the grave about. I used to clean up her father's messes and you see how he is now. I'm not about to do that for Trinity, especially if it hurts others. Trinity was going to make shit right but she died before that could happen." Kimberly handed me her phone with a video ready to be watched.

I looked from Kimberly to the phone as Kimberly shrugged. I pressed play and it showed Trinity's house. I could see Trinity mixing some powder into a glass of water before I emerged out of the bathroom. I drunk the water and it took only a few minutes for me to be slumped on the floor. But what I saw next had me in disbelief. Trap Star and Alisha came out of the back room and helped Trinity drag me up the stairs. I didn't need to see nothing else. My baby mama was so damn crazy. I wish I never met her.

"Trinity sent me this video the day she died. I didn't understand why she would incriminate herself. But I think it was something else going on. Plus, why would she drug you when she was happy with Kevin? My daughter was a lot of things but this was not her thing."

"I got to go." I put Izzy's bag over my shoulder. Trinity was a dumb bitch and I didn't like how her mama was making excuses. I knew I was drugged and now I had the proof. Not only that, it gave me the proof that Jayson had set up his own granddaughter to be kidnapped.

"There's one more thing, Isaiah." Kimberly's voice shook.

"Okay..."

"Izzy isn't your son. I found the paperwork. The real one. He's Tyler's son."

"Tyler? Tyler Richardson?" I needed to sit down as I stared at the paternity paper with the official seal of the state of Florida, unlike the one that was sent to me in the mail. All this time I been taking care of baby that wasn't mine. So much shit could have went better if Trinity would have kept it one hundred with me. She knew that baby wasn't mine from the get-go. I knew I wasn't tripping. I strapped up every time.

"He was Trinity's boyfriend. "

"Wait." I had to get this shit clear. "Trap Star is Isaiah Green Junior's father? Jaya's ex-husband?"

"Trinity was obsessed about Jaya. She for the longest was jealous of her. I think she sought him out just like she sought you out. Like I said, towards the end of her life she was trying to do better. I had no clue that Tyler even knew Jaya until I seen his face on news as the suspect in Israel's disappearance."

"This whole time I thought I was tripping when I would say they look alike. They got the same daddy." I don't think I could take another revelation.

"I'm sorry. And I understand if you don't want to continue in Izzy's life."

I looked down at the paper again. "Its not Izzy's fault. And he still going to be my son."

"Ok." Kimberly patted my shoulder. "I'm here for whatever you need."

"Appreciate it." I replied as prepared to leave.

My mind was all over the place. I didn't know how shit had gone from bad to worse. When Trinity first told me she was pregnant, I was hoping that Izzy was not mine. And now I was hurt that he wasn't mine. But now I knew that I wasn't tripping about not fucking Trinity. Even though Trinity tried to right her wrongs in the end, she had caused so much damage. She knew damn well that Izzy wasn't my baby, hence the fake paternity test results that was sent to me.

As I look back, I didn't approach Trinity, she approached me. She said all the right things. Liked all the shit I liked. She wanted us to be together and I was with it. But what she didn't know was that once Jaya came back no bitch was going to hold my attention. But what I didn't know was why some nigga was so worried about me. He couldn't be just tripping on me about me taking over his blocks. He was making major bread probably more than me.

More than anything I was happy that I had the evidence to prove to Jaya that I wasn't fucking her sister. I just hoped Jaya would believe me. These last few weeks was hard. I ain't had a home cooked meal or no pussy. I wanted my family back.

I called Jaya and she answered on the second ring. "Where you at?" I was anxious.

"I'm at home. Why?"

The shit that bothered me the most was Jaya's level of being unbothered. That first day she found out about Trinity, she fucked up my truck. But after that, she didn't trip. She let me come get Israel, she didn't cuss me out, she was even cordial, like I was someone she never wanted.

"I need come holla at you."

"Not today, Isaiah."

"You got a nigga over there or something?"

"Actually, I do."

"You got a nigga around my daughter?" I jumped off the freeway to Jaya's house.

"Isaiah, I thought we already talked about this. I'm doing me. You're doing you. Look I got to go, I got company and I don't want to be rude. You can come get Israel later if you want to."

"Alright." I tried to hide my anger. "I'll call you later."

"Okay, bet." Jaya hung up her phone.

I was doing ninety to get to her. As soon as pulled up I seen the second car in her driveway, and I was hot. I got Izzy out the car and used my free hand to bang on the door.

"Ice? The fuck?" Jaya swung open the door. "And you brought Izzy? What the hell is wrong with you?"

"Where he at?" I bypassed Jaya to find some man in the living room, papers on table, and Israel in the swing.

"How you doing, man?" The man stood up.

"Did Jaya tell you she had a man?" I knew I didn't look like a threat holding a baby but I had no problem sliding this nigga.

"We are not together!" Jaya shouted. "You can't just come in my house trying to run shit."

"Jay, I'm gonna go." The man looked from me to Jaya.

"Jay?" I looked at this nigga crazy. His ass was being too comfortable.

"Okay, I'll call you later." Jaya replied as the man walked to the door.

"What the fuck, Jaya?"

"Ice, you can't be cheating and then be mad, I'm doing me too."

I didn't like Jaya being so calm. It let me know that maybe I had lost her. "I didn't cheat Jaya."

"I don't want to hear that shit again."

"Trinity drugged me." I showed Jaya my phone.

"Trap Star was there? But why?" Jaya looked confused.

"He's Izzy's daddy."

"But we got the paternity results in the mail." Jaya took Izzy out of my arms. "Why would Trinity lie?"

"At one point she wanted to be you. But I really think that the person that died really changed for the better. She just was doing the most before."

"This shit is crazy. So, you weren't cheating?" Jaya looked at me. "And Izzy is only my nephew?"

"Yeah." I kissed Jaya lightly.

"I don't know what to say." Jaya looked into my eyes.

"Say that you going to come home."

"I can't keep letting some man come in and save the day. All my life. Shawnie. Trap Star. You. I never had to look out for myself. Shit, I dropped out of high school to be the plug's wife. I love you but I got to choose me this time, Ice."

"All this shit we been through..." I was so confused.

"I'm not saying I don't want to be with you. I'm saying that I'm not moving out my house. I need to do this for me and Israel."

I didn't want to hear that. I had fought so hard to be in Jaya's life. I wanted to see us all under one roof. But I was just happy that Jaya was willing to give me another chance. " That's not what I wanted to hear. But I'm on whatever you on."

Jaya smiled. "See this is why I love you so much."

"Can I ask you a favor though?"

"What's up?"

"Can I get a home cooked meal and some pussy?"

Jaya laughed. "I got you. Let me put these babies down for a nap."

"I got them." I took Izzy out her hands and went to go pick up Israel. It took me over an hour for me to get them both asleep, but when I emerged out of Israel's bedroom Jaya had the house smelling good with some smothered hamburgers, mashed potatoes, green beans, cornbread, and baked macaroni and cheese. That shit looked good but not as good as the way Jaya was looking. I grabbed my plate and put it in the microwave.

"You not going to eat?" Jaya questioned as she watched me.

"That's for later." I walked up on her and slid the straps of her tank top down off her shoulders, replacing them with soft kisses.

The nigga in me wanted to rip off her shorts and flip her over and tear that ass up. But the man in me wanted to experience her body like an aged bottle of wine. Jaya didn't speak as I pulled her shirt from over her head. Her skin was so soft, I couldn't get over that shit. God knew what he was doing when he made this one. Because it just wasn't Jaya's looks. It was the person. Her heart, the way she made me laugh. There was nothing like it in this world.

The heat between us was electrifying as my mouth found Jaya's mouth. As soon as my hands touched her body I couldn't stop myself as my hands cupped Jaya's ass.

I lifted her up around my waist and brought her to the couch. Jaya pushed me back and fell back onto the couch as she kissed me on my neck. I allowed her to be the aggressor as Jaya unbuckled my pants and slid down her shorts.

I almost drowned in the pool of her nectar as I stroked deep and slow. Jaya began to moan like a banshee. I was seeing why I couldn't get Jaya off my mind because the way she wailed my name and bounced on my dick had me falling in love even more.

Jaya was knocked out on the couch as I lit into my food. Shit was almost as fire as Jaya's pussy. This is what I needed. I was seeing that home wasn't a place. But rather a person. Jaya was home and as of right now I was going to accept that she wanted to live on her own. But I don't think I could last long without her.

Beep.

Jaya's phone was on the counter of the kitchen letting me know she had gotten a text message. I wasn't the type of nigga that went through my bitch's phone. But when the name Ace flashed across the screen, I grabbed the phone.

Ace: My bad. I was in the shower. I got you, always. But I'll slide thru tomorrow. I hope you like seafood.

But it was the thread from the day that had me wondering if Jay was moving on.

Jaya: My bad about baby daddy.

Ace: If I had someone like you, I would be tripping too. LOL We didn't even get to finish.

Jaya: I know. I really do appreciate everything you're doing.

21

DEJAH

"It's a girl."

"The fuck" Shawnie got angry. "You ain't seeing that big ass dick my son got?"

"Sir, that's the umbilical cord." The ultrasound tech responded. "Your son is a daughter."

"Ain't this about a bitch."

"Seriously?" I looked at Shawnie with disgust. He was so fucking ghetto.

"I didn't want no girls. They too much trouble."

"Well, that's your karma for all the women you did dirty." I rolled my eyes.

The tech just looked at us like we were toxic.

"You wilding. You know I'ma love my baby regardless."

"You better."

"Umm, I will give y'all a minute. Please speak with the front desk about scheduling another appointment." The tech looked at us before leaving.

"Are you really upset about us having a girl?"

"Hell fucking yeah. I've been surrounded by girls all my life. They be too emotional. The way I used to knock down bitches? I don't want no nigga fucking my daughter."

"Well, what do you want me to do? Send it back?'

"Nah, man." Shawnie rubbed my belly. "I'm feeling a type of way. But I'm happy for us."

"Let's just go." I was upset and ready to go home.

"So what, I'm not allowed to say how I feel?"

"If you want to start an argument Shawnie, just say that."

"Whatever man."

"So what's the problem?"

"You going to the house?" Shawnie's eyes turned cold.

All day, Shawnie has been acting distant and off. I know Shawnie wanted a son but the way he was reacting to having a daughter was all uncalled for. I just didn't want to argue with him, I just wanted to go home.

"Whatever."

As soon as I got into the door I went to our bedroom and laid down. My mind was swimming in my thoughts of why Shawnie was acting like this.

"I'll be back later tonight." Shawnie stood in the door of our bedroom.

"What's later?" I sat up.

"Later."

"Who is she? Keisha?"

"Why you always accusing me of cheating? And I'm tired of hearing about Keisha. If you that insecure why you marry me?"

"Because I love you. Because I thought you loved me too."

"I do. I just got a lot going on."

"Like?"

"Its nothing. I got it handled."

"So where are you going?"

"To Keisha's..."

"Well at least you being honest about cheating on your pregnant wife. Thank you."

"I'm not cheating. I'm picking up my niece."

"Okay. I will be in the car." I stood.

"I don't think that's a good idea." Shawnie grabbed me by the arm. "I'm not trying have no drama. I'ma have my mom get her. I'm feeling boxed in, Dejah."

"Wow."

"Its not you. Its family shit. Shit I don't want you involved in. The less you know the better. So if the police come asking questions you can't tell them nothing. I'll be back." Shawnie kissed my cheek, not giving me time to react.

I woke to hear Shawnie on the phone but when he seen that I was up he told Ice he will hit him back.

"I did some thinking. And with everything that we been through it's not fair for me to keep secrets from you. I'm not selling drugs no more. I will never do that shit again. I'm just helping Ice run money through a couple laundry mats."

At this point I rather Shawnie had said he was cheating. At least he wouldn't be risking his freedom. I wasn't even angry but disappointed. I did the last few months with Shawnie when he was in prison. I couldn't handle it then and now being his wife and the mother of his child, I know I couldn't do it.

"So, you're going to risk your freedom? What about us?"

"Ice is my bro. This shit is temporary and I know if I was in his situation he would have my back."

"And what if you get caught? I don't want to bring our daughter to see her dad in jail."

"I know."

"We are fine financially. We are not hurting for..."

"I said I know!" Shawnie snapped. "I'ma tell him I'm out." Shawnie didn't look my way.

"I just want us to be..." My sentence was cut short as a pain shot through my back. "Aww!" I yelped.

"Baby you bleeding!" Shawnie pointed out as I looked and saw the crimson liquid seeping through my shorts.

I was only five months pregnant, meaning I was too far along for a miscarriage but just in the range for a stillborn. "The baby. I can't lose her."

"We ain't going to." Shawnie reached for me to help me off the bed. Shawnie was trying to keep the mood calm but I could see the fear in his eyes as he sped to Jackson Memorial.

"Baby I'm sorry for how I been acting. I'm sorry for being upset about our daughter." Shawnie said.

"Its okay." I gritted down on my teeth as the pain hit me again. It seemed like every five minutes the pain came back. I was praying like crazy for God to save my baby. All I wanted was to hold my daughter, but not like this.

The car was barely in park as Shawnie picked me up and ran me into the emergency room. I was in so much pain I didn't even care if anybody saw my bloody shorts. We didn't have to wait for a nurse. It only took a matter of seconds before I was being placed on gurney.

The pain was getting stronger and I found myself getting sleepy. "Sir you can't come back here!" I heard someone yell at Shawnie.

"Nigga you got me fucked up! That's my wife."

The nurses and doctors began to work fast as an oxygen mask went over my face and they began to hook me up to an IV and some monitors.

I guess nobody wanted to go toe to toe with Shawnie and the medical staff allowed him to hold my hand as they ran me down the hall. The urge to take a nap was getting stronger as I was rushed into a surgical room. Shawnie refused to leave me and security had to be called to remove him. I was warm and numb and had no desire to react.

"She's coding!" Were the last words Shawnie heard before being escorted away. It was the last words I heard too as my eyes got heavy and I succumbed to the sleepiness that took over my being.

22

KEISHA

"If only your Mama could see you right now." I smiled at Sidney as I admired the pristine white Milla Nova wedding dress she was wearing. The white gold tiara with purple sapphires and green emeralds accented the soft ringlets pinned to the right side of her head. Sidney took a deep breath as Bernard placed the French silk veil over her face. She looked so lovely as radiance emitted from her aura as Bernard took Sidney's arm into his to head to the courtyard for the ceremony.

I was happy to be a part of this amazing day and I was honored that Sidney wanted me to be here, even though her ass was only a few years younger than me. Sidney's mother died when she was younger and I was more than happy to stand in her mother's place. I was finally at a place in my life where I was happy and Bernard and Sidney had become my family.

Sidney was trying to remain calm but here she was about to marry the man she had known for the majority of her life. Just the thought of it had me thinking of Shawnie. This could have been us. But he moved on and so had I.

I watched Sidney try to get her emotions in control but Jhene Aiko was singing her heart out in the song "While We're

Young" and when she finally laid eyes on her fiancé she was a crying mess.

I imagined myself walking down the aisle one day. I tried to imagine it being Bernard, but my mind wouldn't let me as I couldn't stop picturing Shawnie. Standing at the alter stood the man that had shaped me into the strong woman that I had become. The father of my future beautiful chocolate hued babies. The man that I fought abuse, rape, and depression to see again. The man that would go to war with the devil behind me. The man who willing walked away from a multi-million-dollar drug industry for me. The man that possessed my heart. And more importantly, the man that simply made me feel like the world could be safe again. My imaginary wedding ended as I focused back on the real wedding.

You know I'm down to ride
I'm giving you my heart, please don't break it
Take it and lock it up and put me in your pocket, love
Alright, right by your side
I'll go everywhere you go
You know I'll go, I'll go
Everywhere you go
Baby while we're young

The courtyard of the Versace House Mansion was absolutely beautiful. Money was not an option as Bernard dropped over one hundred thousand dollars on the wedding, honeymoon, and flying out his family from Texas for five days of festivities that led up to the wedding. The courtyard was vibrant with lush purple and lime green orchids and other tropical flowers flown in from the Bahamas.

As a matter of fact, the entire wedding was tropical themed. The Versace House had a strict policy to only use their in-house catering. But Sidney wanted authentic Caribbean food, so her aunts were cooking jerk meats, mango salsas, fruit salads, peas and rice, and other popular island food.

The aisle was lined with large bouquets of purple and green flowers, almost identical to Sidney's bouquet. Only difference is that the flower jewelry in the line stalks were Swarovski crystals and Sidney's were real tear drop diamonds. An array of green trick dianthus, white anemones, purple peonies, green cymbidium orchids, and purple calla lilies, costing almost three thousand for the bouquet alone.

Sidney looked into her fiancé's teary eyes as she began her vows, "I Sidney, can't imagine life without you. The whole time I was gone all I could do was think about you. I haven't had much experience in the love department. You have been my only love. But what I do know is that only a dope boy can love me. You have sacrificed so much and with every breath within in me and I will always show you how much I'm grateful. Because of you, I laugh, I smile, I dare to dream again. I look forward with great joy to spending the rest of my life with you, caring for you, nurturing you, being there for you in all life has for us, and I vow to be true and faithful for as long as we both shall live."

Patrick had tears in his eyes and it reminded me of how Shawnie would look at me. "I call you 'My Queen' because you are my everything. You are my light and you've shown me more love than I've ever known. You know me better than anyone else in this world and somehow still you manage to love me. You are my best friend and one true love. There is still a part of me today that cannot believe that I'm the one who gets to marry you. You have been my best friend, mentor, playmate, confidant, and my greatest challenge. But most importantly, you are the love of my life and you make me happier than I could ever imagine and more loved than I ever thought possible... You have made me a better person, as our love for one another is reflected in the way I live my life. So I am truly blessed to be a part of your life, which as of today becomes our life together."

Sidney's fiancé with forced confidence finished his vows as his nerves had the best of him.

The minister with a smile announced. "Please join me in introducing Mr. and Mrs. Patrick Young!"

Everyone let out cheers as the newlyweds made their way back down the aisle.

Gucci Mane and Keyshia's reception looked like a homeless shelter compared to the extravagance of Sidney and Patrick's reception. The interior walls were draped with large green and purple shimmering cloth. Behind the wedding party table was a large gobo that read "Patrick & Sidney." Birds of paradise and white and purple orchids were placed in three-foot water filled vase centerpieces to imitate tropical trees. On the food table each Caribbean dish was place on top of large palm leaves. But the real beauty was the cake. A seven-foot cake adorned with purple and green orchids, an edible cake crystal to mimic diamonds, emeralds, and purple sapphires. Each seven tiers had a different flavor with the bottom having the shape of the Jamaican flag when cut into. In total, Bernard spent two million on the reception alone.

All two thousand of the guests were in silence as 50 dancers dressed in green, black and yellow majorette costumes and elaborate carnival headdresses filled into the ballroom. Dancehall music began to play and the dancers came to life as they went into full carnival mode. Everybody was in awe as the 50 dancers moved like one. As quickly as they began they divided into two groups creating a walkway. They death dropped to the floor forming an aisle with their headdresses. The song changed again to "While we are young" Sidney and Patrick's theme song for the wedding. Emerged Patrick and Sidney dressed in Caribbean Carnival themed clothing. Sidney wore a provocative and body forming one piece with a flowing long open skirt and purple and green head dress more extravagant than the dancers. She looked like a Caribbean princess as Patrick lead her down the aisle of dancers.

The commotion of Sidney and Patrick walking into the reception area had died down and people began to dance and eat.

"Can I have everybody's attention?" I heard Bernard speak from the DJs booth. But all eyes were on me as the big spotlight landed on me. "Baby, there are many ways to be happy in this life, but all I really need is you. When I look into your eyes, I can see a reflection of the two of us and the life I hope we'll share together. I know my life will never be complete without you beside me to share it. When I look into my heart, I see only you. Keisha Nicole Johnson, will you take a gamble on this old man and be my wife?"

No this nigga didn't. We had only been dating for a short time. But I didn't want to embarrass him in front of his whole family. This spotlight was hot as fuck as everybody waited for my answer. "Bernard, I love you.." I smiled. "You make me so happy..."

❦ 23 ❦

TIA

"Wow look who finally comes and sees me."

I rolled my eyes and sat down.

"You still fine as fuck, T." Jayson admired what he seen in front of him.

"Back off of Isaiah, Jayson. You know I ain't fucking with you. Shit been over between us."

"You think I'm tripping about some pussy I ain't had in over twenty years? Let's talk about the fact that you had me thinking Isaiah was my son."

"I told you from the get-go that I didn't know if you or Alejandro was the father."

I had so many secrets. For one I been knowing Jayson for a long time. I met him in Cuba when I was fifteen and he was twenty and I let this nigga game me. I was so in love that we got married after two months. Jayson isolated me by moving me out of Havana where my parents were to across the island to Santigo de Cuba. I was fifteen years old getting my ass whopped. I was making excuses for a sociopath that didn't give a fuck about me.

I was hiding the black eyes from my parents when I would visit them. I made it seem like Jayson was the love of my life, because that's what I felt. One night, I was at the bar and I got too drunk and ended up sleeping with this Cuban man. I didn't tell Jayson about the Cuban man until my belly started to grow. I laid up in the hospital for over a week. My eye was swollen shut and I had two broken ribs. I lied and said I got robbed. When I watched Jayson cry real tears to the policia about how sad he was that his pregnant wife got robbed, I knew that I was married to the devil.

But every time I tried to leave, Jayson would say that I gave up on him like everybody else did. And my naïve ass would go back. I didn't see the wrong until I moved back to the US, pregnant and thinking that the move would make shit better for me and my husband.

I was hoping that my first born was his. But when Isaiah came out light and didn't darken up like Jayson and me, he beat my ass. He hit me so hard that I dropped Isaiah. Then he hit me harder for dropping Isaiah. Blaming me for taking his chance away from being a father. I didn't learn until Isaiah was one years old that he divorced Kimberly only two days before we got married and that he already had Trinity.

I was so scared of Jayson that I sent a letter, along with the divorce decree to him so that I could be free. I moved on with my life, hoping to never lay eyes on Jayson again. But when Isaiah told me that he was dealing with Shawnie's uncle and then I found out it was Jayson, I was pissed. I didn't even tell Isaiah that I knew Jayson. I knew it would cause so many issues. When I found that Trinity was Jayson's daughter, I knew it would bring nothing but turmoil to my only son. That's why I gave him the green light to kill the bitch if shit went left. I didn't feel the same about Jaya. Because she wasn't like Trinity and Jayson. Even though that was her father I knew that Jaya wasn't grimy.

I wanted to protect my son as much as possible. That's why I told him that I would handle it. For one I knew how calculating Jayson was and I didn't want Isaiah to know my connection to Jayson.

"You wouldn't be no fucking plug if wasn't for me. I'm sitting here because of you. This ain't about no pussy. This purely revenge. Bando is a dead nigga."

"Revenge? You killed his dad. You killed that woman. And those are the murders they know about. What about Kimberly's dad? And no telling who else. You are the reason why you are here."

"His daddy killed Maya, T!"

"Ashton killed Jaya's mama?" I referred to Bando's dad. I didn't know that. I changed my number and any letter that came to my house I never opened. When I said I was done with Jayson, I meant that shit. By the time Isaiah was two years old, I had broke free of Jayson's abuse. Before he went to prison I heard he had another child, but I was long gone living my life.

"Yeah. Look I know I was a horrible husband. I'm sorry. I was young and stupid. But this ain't about us no more. I didn't want Ice fucking with my daughter because I thought he was working with Bando. But I learned that's not true. Bando had my granddaughter kidnapped. He killed my daughter and he been hitting all Ice's spots. I need you to do this for me, T."

"You know I can't." I looked at Jayson like he lost his mind. He really was crazy. When I found out that Jayson was cheating on me with Jaya's mama. I broke up with him. Miami was so small and I only learned about how Jaya being Jayson's daughter in the last year. I knew that she had a father that was doing time, but I didn't look into it. I wish I would have. "I will deal with Bando myself. Just leave my son the fuck alone."

"I don't think I can do that, T. I been fronting him helluvz\a bread. Bando been hitting all his spots."

I grabbed my head in frustration. I had no idea that shit was this bad. And I was hurt that Isaiah couldn't come to me with the truth, rather than blaming Jayson.

"You know you still got feelings for me. But you got to stop thinking I'm the enemy."

"Nigga I ain't Maya or Kimberly. And I definitely not that

scary ass bitch you was beating on in Cuba." I referred to the girl I used to be.

Jayson smiled. "You miss me? You know you will always be the love of my life. Isaiah really should have been mine."

"Well he's not. You ain't going to like what I do if you keep this shit up. You hurting your daughter too by getting into it with Bando. This shit is all your fault. If some shit happens to my son, you already know–"

"Fuck Bando. I tried to come to understanding. I killed his dad because he killed my baby mama. Ashton took Maya away from my daughter. Bando don't want no truce. And I don't give a fuck about my life but my daughter is all I got. He already took Trinity, I can't lose Jaya. He put the hit out for my daughter and cried at her funeral. You think I give a fuck about your threats? You know me better than that."

I knew Jayson was capable of a lot of shit but I wish Bando and he would leave Isaiah out of it. I don't give a fuck who these niggas killed. They weren't going to continue fuck with mine.

"You been warned." I stood to leave.

"What's the saying, T? If they can't get to you they will go after your baby. You took over my blocks. Didn't send me a dime from my own dope. Took the chance for me have a son, and you broke my heart. It's only fair that you help me."

I fucking lost it as I dove over the metal table to hit Jayson. I was no longer the scary bitch and I had hands. All the pain he brought me, had resurfaced. But Jayson didn't even swing back. Even when the guards came over to restrain me, I was trying to kill this nigga.

"I miss you too, Tia." Jayson lifted my chin. "But you we are past talking to Bando. You going to have to choose between your baby brother and your son."

"Nigga fuck your heart. I'm not helping with shit. Stop contacting my son!" I yelled as the guards held my arms.

Jayson laughed. "Bring it, T. I will be seeing you real soon. You know you miss how I used to pipe you down. You never forget your first." Jayson kissed my lips. "I love you. Give me a few weeks and I'm come holla at you."

I was stunned from Jayson's calmness that I couldn't move. I was scared for my baby. This wasn't even his battle and some how my refusal to not get involved with my ex-husband and my baby's brother's beef had Isaiah stuck in the crosshairs.

Jayson looked at me one more time and smiled before walking back to his cell.

"Stay the fuck away from my son!" I screamed at Jayson's back.

Don't worry, T. I'm coming for Bando. Little brother or not." Jayson said over his shoulder.

The End...for now.

Part 3, the finale, coming soon.